Gift From The Sea

P.K. Glaser

Acknowledgments

Rebecca, thank you for being my cheerleader and giver of encouragement, and for letting me know that this is indeed a possibility! Angel, thank you for making the time to read the baby version of my story. Thank you, Joe, for letting me read out loud and fumble through my editing. Jacob, Sheila, and Alliah, thank you for being examples to me on how to take chances and go after dreams.

Also thank you so much to the team at BakeMyBook.com for holding my hand through the process and helping to make me and the book look so good.

Prologue

BEFORE MEMORY, there was Calypso, ruling below the ocean's depths, encircling the majority of the earth. There she and her children thrived and learned. With the pull of the moon and the heat of the sun, the earth shook and trembled, often changing its face. Dry land grew as the oceans shrank, with more and more shorelines developing. Calypso knew it was time for her children to stretch and grow, to learn the things they could only learn beyond their brackish borders. Two-thirds of her children were to leave their watery home while one-third stayed behind.

She watched as the bravest of her children pulled themselves up on the sandy, rocky shores to experience the weight of gravity and the feeling of air in their developing lungs. There was one son, in particular, her dearest son, although she would not admit it to the others that she kept a particular eye on. He and his descendants never traveled too far from the shore.

Generations came and went as mortality was part of their growth. Calypso watched the descendants of her darling son approvingly for many generations as they discovered their new world in equal portions to what they forgot of their beginnings. As their fight for physical survival became easier, they developed intellectually. Here they learned to become vain and proud. Still, she watched.

No matter how far her children journeyed and settled towards the lands beyond, they were always called back to the sea. The sea fed them physically and emotionally, always calmed by its shores. The desire to know and conquer the sea drove them to design and build vessels of increasing size and capacity.

Soon her children found her other children that had crawled up on the shores of other lands, and their world grew exponentially.

It is after this time that we focus on the descendants of her darling son.

The girl was beautiful, that was true enough; spoiled but not mean-spirited, often acting without thought to consequences. Her father traveled over the sea regularly for his business and provided handsomely for his beloved daughter and wife. For all his time gone, he would indulge his loving daughter a little more than he should have, but it was only because he loved her so much. Her mother was a gentle woman who had wanted nothing more than a loving husband and beautiful daughter; which she conceived after some difficulty, so she considered herself quite blessed and didn't have it in her to ever truly reprimand the child. Of course, the girl was not entirely awful; she was quite generous in many ways. She often spoke her mind as she had always been encouraged by her parents, but hadn't quite acquired the proper restraint or etiquette such candor sometimes requires.

1

"**D**ADDY!" SHE EXCLAIMED, quickly descending the curving grand staircase that greeted many important guests over the years, holding up her abundant layers of taffeta and lace, her shoes making a soft click-click-click on the white marble steps.

Carrie Ann watched her beloved daughter rush down the stairs thinking she should remind her that ladies do not raise their voices, nor do they proceed at such an uncomely pace down the stairs, or anywhere for that matter.

Sebastian's business of land acquisition had taken him overseas. He had been gone longer than expected. Naturally, his wife and daughter missed him terribly. The daughter adored her father and the feelings of the father towards the daughter were quite mutual.

Leaping into her father's embrace, even though she was getting much too big for it, Sebastian braced himself taking her into his arms, enjoying every moment of it, realizing his daughter was reaching adulthood and soon he would no longer have these moments. He reveled in her excitement as she had a thousand questions tumbling out at once.

"Tonight, my darling, tonight. We will talk all about it tonight. For now, I must see to some final business before I can settle in. I promise we will visit tonight."

At the dinner table, the family discussed the plans for a dance and social they would need to host. Servants wove in and out flawlessly furtive, attending to the family's needs. A party was imperative for advertising Sebastian's success in hopes of recruiting potential clients.

After dinner had been served and the dishes cleared away without notice, the family retired to the sitting room before an established warm fire awaiting after-dinner drinks and tea. Following a moment of relaxed quiet, Carrie Ann watched, amused as their daughter became more fidgety, her pretense of decorum wearing thin. Their daughter could pretend disinterest no longer, bursting out,

"Oh Daddy, I just cannot wait another moment! What did you bring me, silly goose?"

"I'm sorry my darling, I found nothing divine enough for my princess on this trip. Although I looked and looked, there was nothing that shone as bright as you."

With the most wounded pout she could muster, and a droop of her right shoulder, the daughter replied, in an efficiently dismayed voice, "Please don't tease, Daddy."

Sebastian, never a match for that maneuver, gave a sigh then a giggle signaling with a snap and a wave to the awaiting manservant standing dutifully near the door. Accepting a beautifully wrapped box from the bowing man Sebastian, in turn, presented it to his daughter. She expelled a small squeal of excitement as she carefully untied the silk bow, thinking she could save that for her ladies' maid. Even an inferior packaging bow would be a delight to her.

The box contained a lovely light blue velvet pair of shoes with ethereal hand-embroidered flowers in multiple shades of blues and lavender. Crystal beadwork and small gems were elegantly worked into the design. They were her first pair of shoes with a bit of heel on them seeing as she was now considered to be a young woman.

"Oh Father, they are exquisite. Mother, have you seen these? Aren't they the most beautiful thing you have ever seen?"

"There is a dress and ribbons to match darling, waiting in your room." Carrie Ann responded, delighting in her daughter's delight. "Shall we retire? We have an early day with much to ready for the social, and I believe you are ready to help me with the planning my dearest, aren't you?"

"Oh yes! I will offer a piece on the grand and a song! I'm sure that will delight everybody, don't you agree, Daddy?" their most treasured daughter offered as she kissed them both from cheek to cheek and swished towards the door.

The guests arrived in their finest carriages, some hired for a better first impression. To be successful, you need to seem successful already. Power and the appearance of power were of utmost importance, all the while appearing effortless and inconsequential.

Standing at the top of the stairs to be seen better, the daughter scanned the arrivals for her friend Lidia. Lidia's father often accompanied Sebastian on business trips to help 'persuade the poor ignorant heathens' that it was in their best interest to sell their land. After all, what did they know about truly making the most of the land and using it to its best potential? They needed intellectually superior businessmen to show them how to fully take advantage of the land they lived on. In return, they would be allowed to live and work there, receiving a fair wage. How could they possibly understand the intricacies of business and finance? They had to be shown the benefits of doing more than just existing when there was profit to be made.

Spying Lidia as she entered, the daughter waved frantically from the top of the stairs to gain her attention. She needn't of course, Lidia always knew right where to find her friend at these functions, right where she could be well seen by all who attended. Joining her friend dutifully, staying one step below and to the side so as not to block the guest's view of the hosts' daughter, Lidia knew her place beside her.

Sebastian and Carrie Ann beamed up at their beloved daughter Olivia, as she chose the perfect moment to descend the stairs making her official entrance for the evening. Lidia followed, careful to stay one step behind as they joined the crowd of guests and began to mingle.

One guest, in particular, stood out amongst the others. Captain Bankman. Not so much for his stature or looks but despite them. He was older and corpulent. His face was ruddy and round, pocked with scars possibly from adolescence. What drew your attention mostly to the captain though was, the fact that he still insisted on wearing a rather tall off-white powdered wig, a fashion long since abandoned by most men and women. Adding to the look was the powder he continued wearing on his face that did nothing to hide the ruddiness. Notwithstanding the antiquated captain's jacket and breeches, finished with his shiny elevated shoes. Those who knew him abode the man his vanities because he carried a degree of influence in the shipping and commerce circles. The Bankman family was old blood carrying with it a measure of repute and respect. Yet he was still considered a necessary evil, arrogant, rude and entitled as allowed by his derivation.

Hors d'oeuvres and drinks were served as the guests made small talk and connections. Olivia had noticeably caught the eye of Captain Bankman. The last time he had seen her, she had not yet begun to blossom, still evidencing a hint of the woman she would become in time. He couldn't help but notice that time had arrived and worked diligently throughout the evening to keep her in his line of sight.

Sebastian lightly struck his glass to quiet the conversations and gain their guests' attention. "Everybody, friends, it is so good to have you all in attendance and see you all so well. Carrie Ann and I would like to invite you to join us in the conservatory for a special treat before we assemble in the ballroom for the dancing part of the evening. Our precious Olivia has agreed to gift us all with an entertainment of song!"

Captain Bankman stood indifferently to one side of the room near the french doors during the performance, smoking his cigar with a small number of the other men. He was completely taken by Olivia and was quite sure he had never heard anything quite as exquisite as her voice or her playing. Her voice and talent were admirable to be sure, if not exaggerated in Captain Bankman's appraisal.

After her song, followed by gracious applause, the party continued with dancing in the ballroom with a quartet performing in the corner. Olivia was not wanting for dance partners and passed a number of them along to Lidia. Many of the young attendees were the youth Olivia and Lidia had grown up with at these soirees.

Eventually, Captain Bankman made his way to Olivia and offered her his hand as a way of asking for a dance. Without thought, Olivia looked at his outstretched hand then at his particularly tall off-white wig, and laughed despite herself. Captain Bankman flushed, turning his face a deeper shade of blotchy but remained standing, hand held out.

"Oh! My apologies Captain Bankman. I'm feeling quite besot suddenly and believe I must get some fresh air. If you'll forgive me." Olivia quickly excused herself as she grabbed Lidia by the hand, ineffectually suppressing a giggle, and escaped to their favorite spot to sit and visit, away from the adults.

Normally they would have waited until after the dancing wound down, the men retired to the study for final nightcaps and cigars, the women to the library for sherry and cards, but this seemed as good a time as any to make their escape. Normally Olivia enjoyed socializing and entertaining guests as well as receiving the attention that was so easily obtained, but Captain Bankman's attention was too much. She had indeed noticed his eyes on her all evening and had endured about enough of that gentleman's unwanted leering.

2

REACHING THE THIRD FLOOR, Olivia and Lidia walked amicably arm in arm down the long hallway flanked by doors belonging to several guest rooms. All would eventually be filled before dawn as many guests traveled quite a distance to attend this important assembly.

The hall ended with an impressive wall of windows centered with another set of grand french doors the width of four people and half that high. Stepping through the great doors emptying onto the stone balcony, both girls took deep revitalizing breaths enjoying the familiar scent of the ocean. Leaning against the cool rail perched atop curved marble balusters, the friends paused to take in their well-regarded view. The night sky was clear, revealing a waning moon still half full and casting a radiant light on the calm waters. The salty air was a welcome relief from the stuffy smells of perfumed bodies, smoke, and arrangements.

Olivia took her place in one of the soft upholstered lounging chairs, indicating that Lidia should light the two oil lanterns hanging on either side of the balcony before Olivia took her place in the lounging chair beside her.

"Can you believe that Captain Bankman?" Olivia eagerly began, "Somebody really should counsel him about that ridiculous wig he wears. I know they used to be the fashion when he was younger but that was so very long ago. And then when he asked me to dance! I'm so glad I was able to use the excuse of being tired, I wouldn't have wanted to lie."

"You certainly weren't short of dance partners this evening, Olivia. The gentlemen were queuing up for a turn on the floor with you." Lidia flattered her in all sincerity.

"Indeed," Olivia continued, "I did try to turn a few your way, Lidia, not that you weren't getting some offers on your own. You are such a good dancer and so lovely in your way. I do sometimes wish that they would direct some of that attention aimed at me towards you, that they could see you how I see you. You are so dear."

Lidia knew better than to be offended by Olivia's seemingly thoughtless remarks and was just thinking that very thing to herself when both girls were startled by a huge splash from the waters below. It was a calm and quiet night outside the manor, and the noise took them by surprise. Stretching along their lounge chairs to see if they could spot what the noise had been, they only saw the trace of ripples most likely created by a rather large fish breaching. Those sightings were rare on this stretch of shallow shore; Olivia could only remember a handful of occasions when there was evidence of a larger creature coming so close. Those sightings had been accompanied by fanciful stories of a Sea Siren or Selkie spotted by local fishermen.

In their curiosity and shifting in their chairs, Lidia's skirts hiked above her ankles drawing Olivia's attention to her friend's new shoes for the first time that evening, a lovely soft lavender-colored leather, tied with velvet laces all upon a delicate heel.

"Lidia, those are lovely shoes. They compliment your dress so well. Not quite a perfect match, but complimentary nonetheless. Look at the ones Daddy brought home for me." She declared, sliding her foot slightly forward into the light, tilting her foot this way and that so the jewels caught the light.

"Those are amazing, Olivia! I've never seen anything like them." Lidia's reply was met with a delighted squeal from Olivia.

"I know! They match my dress perfectly, and did you see," turning her head left to right "I had my lady's maid plait the matching ribbon through my hair. Did you notice?"

So they continued gossiping about the boys they grew up with, who was the most handsome, or of a better position, about the girls and their dresses and of course shoes, who would suit who for marriage amongst them, and so on until their mothers found them in their favorite spot. The girls' mothers' hated to disappoint them with the news that Lidia and her family were ready to leave for home and Olivia should ready herself for bed also.

Sebastian and Carrie Ann joined their daughter in her chambers after the lady's maids had helped her into her nightclothes, removed all the ribbons and braids from her thick dark curls, combing them through, and readied her for bed. The far window was open, allowing the ever-present scent of the sea to dance around the room, twirling with the light, smoky from the evening's fire entwined with the bergamot of Olivia's lotion.

Perched at the side of her bed, her father started, "Darling, I've acquired another business opportunity this evening as hoped. Only this one must be attended to quickly, and I'll be leaving in three days."

"Oh Daddy, no. You've only just returned and my birthday is coming! Must you go?" Olivia protested with her signature pout, the sad upturned eyes, slightly protruding lower lip, and droop of her right shoulder. "I'll just die if you leave so soon. Send somebody else. Mommy, can't you make him stay? I can't stand the idea!"

To which her mother implored, "Now Olivia, my darling girl, please don't upset yourself. You'll have bad dreams my precious, and I can't bear to think of it. We'll see what we can do. Please don't upset yourself, my beloved blessing."

Sebastian and Carrie Ann looked helplessly at one another. What could they do? They never were able to deny their daughter.

A distant splash of water sounded through the open window recovering them from their private thoughts.

Reassuring Olivia that they would find a solution, they tucked her in, kissed her forehead, and went to bed themselves wondering how they would meet their daughter's request.

3

OLIVIA COULDN'T BE more pleased or excited when her father informed her he was able to convince the captain to let her and Carrie Ann join them on the trip. She had no idea of the convincing it took because the captain of the ship they would be sailing on was none other than Captain Bankman, taking a lot of persuading on Sebastian's behalf to convince the man. Captain Bankman was still nursing the sting from the night of the dance. Add to that the long-held superstition of having women on board.

So it will come as no surprise that Olivia may have wanted to reconsider her later behavior toward the proud and vain captain of the large ship. After all, it's not usually a good idea to tell a man of such narcissistic ideas that the invitation to lunch with him on his unnecessarily *large* ship is declined due to the fact that you consider him over-powerful and over-dressed; not to mention his wig being too tall.

Olivia felt that somebody ought to tell him and it might as well be her. Nobody else was going to, and she was doing him a favor after all. He needed to know what others thought of him.

She and her parents, much to their embarrassment, for they had a long trip still ahead, were sent to their cabin sure that they would not be invited to another captain's dinner (or luncheon) for the remainder of the voyage due to the captain's bruised ego. Claire's impertinence would prove inconvenient for the father, to say the least. He dealt with the captain of this ship regularly for his excursions across the sea attending business, and did not wish for their relationship to be strained. He had to convince the captain to allow him to bring his wife and daughter along on this trip in the first place, saying that his wife was a quiet and reserved woman of whom he would barely notice her presence and that his daughter was now a lovely and delightful young woman and as part of her education would do well to see the world on the other side of the sea, not to mention that the father agreed to pay a liberal fee for their accommodations.

Resultantly, the father and mother implored their daughter to apologize to the good captain for the sake of congeniality through the remainder of the journey and future opportunities, for it was the largest ship and the best captain on this side of the sea. Never had they been overtaken by pirates or caused to tip due to the displeasure of the great sea goddess Calypso. For Calypso was always at any ship's side listening, and the proud and vain captain was always sure to sing her praises and send her offerings over the bow of the ship when he was in private because beneath that too tall wig and too much powder, he was still a superstitious cabin boy working under his own hardened father (as often is the case in the face of such bravado).

"But Father, Mother," Olivia argued, admiring her new shoes, putting on her perfected pout indicating that she did not understand why this was even an issue, "why would you even care to dine with that man? Truly, his powder makes my nose tickle! I don't think I could look away from that silly wig of his and I may even find myself giggling."

"My beloved daughter," the father implored, "if you could just bring yourself to apologize we could henceforth claim you are ill from the sea and you wouldn't have to ever eat with him. Your mother and I would go and you could eat here in peace."

"Father, he is an arrogant man and I don't like the way he speaks down to you and mother. He treats his hired hands like mere cattle."

You see, she was not a mean-spirited person, and she recognized right from wrong. Her parents were well at teaching her the golden rules, but as they wanted to keep her life filled with nothing but loveliness, she was quite naive about the ways of the world. She did not understand that sometimes the bullies seemed to win and that decent people often had to resort to white lies or flattery to accomplish their goals in the politics of a world that often, but not always, seemed to reward the greedy and the inconsiderate. Not all understand that what seems to be on the outside doesn't always reflect what is within.

Nonetheless, the parents did try to shield her from the ugliness of the world, but we are not here to point out and blame, for who could fault them, they did love her so.

"I would just as soon like to dine with the smelly fish under the sea than with that man! In fact, I do wish he would get swallowed up by this same sea, him and his beloved *large* ship and too tall wig!" she exclaimed to a gasping mother and father, for Olivia often got what she wished for, although she usually wished for pretty ribbons, new shoes, and tasty treats.

This occasion would be no different, for Calypso was listening at the side of the ship. Olivia had descended from Calypso's favorite son, and Calypso had been watching her lineage with interest. She heard the girl's wish and it amused her greatly, having lived as long as the sea itself and seen many ships come and go riding many tides to and fro. Death meant nothing to her; it was just the passing from one adventure to the next.

And so it was, she decided then and there to grant the girl's wish.

The sea started to rise back and forth, tipping the ship from side to side, Captain Bankman was caught unaware due to the bruised ego he was trying to repair with more powder and fancier shoes. Being a great captain, he had gathered a worthy crew, and they set to the sails and the riggings and all the other seaworthy things, but it mattered not, for Calypso always had her way, and she was determined to bring that ship down.

Being the mother of many great sea creatures she also had compassion for the loving parents of the girl. She arranged it so that they were hit in the head with an errant boom and sent unconscious over the side of the ship early in the misadventure, so they did not have to fear for their daughter's safety long, and down they went into the waters.

The girl on the other hand saw her parents go overboard and felt the first terror of her life. All went silent in her mind, for it was more than she could conceive. Needless to say, she did not notice the rumble of the wooden barrels as they let loose and rolled towards her back. Nor did she notice that she hit her head on one of those barrels after her feet with the beautiful new shoes went flying out beneath her. Nor did she notice that same said barrels carried her along as they headed towards the side of the boat and flung her right over the side into the swirling, cold waters to dine with the smelly fish under the sea.

4

I T WAS LIKE waking from a dream. You know that moment when you are aware you are solid and the weight of the world feels proper around you, though you sense you are still merely observing.

"What is this wrapped around my face and neck? I can't see, I can't breathe!" she thought, grabbing at the clingy, string-like annoyance around her face.

"It's hair!" she realized as she pulled a handful forcefully away *"Ouch! It's mine! That's a pretty color I'd think. Red? Blonde? Brown? Hard to tell,"* her random thoughts swirling irrationally.

"What is this? Am I in my nightgown? No. It seems like a dress… I would never wear these boring colors. Shouldn't there be more fabric for a dress… A nightgown. Funny, I don't remember falling asleep… falling…"

With these abstractions going quickly through her mind, she thought she saw – but everything was so murky still – an elaborately dressed man with a very tall white wig floated by.

"Funny things to wear for a swim and why would a man put on such silly hair? Hair? Air! AIR!!! I NEED AIR!"

Instinctively she started kicking, trying to procure the surface for she knew now that she was drowning, a flash of reality as sharp as the pain in her chest.

"Look for the light. I can't find the light, what way is up? Go towards the surface, kick!" trying not to panic further.

Breaking the water's surface, she tried to gasp in a great gulp of air, only to find that her lungs would not allow it. She began to sink again back to her murky dream. Stubbornly she kicked for the surface again, barely touching the light. Exhausted, past caring, she saw a dark shape coming at her. Still, she was beyond fear at this point, merely curious about how this would play out, again the observer.

Two arms reached around her and she was being pulled and carried at the same time; no effort was needed on her behalf which was good because she found that she was suddenly and completely quite tired.

"Just sleep," she thought, and it did seem perfectly logical to do so until she became unexpectedly aware that something was pressing on her chest, strongly encouraging her to wake. Then she was sure, although she hadn't any reference she could think of, that there were possibly lips pressed to hers, with a feeling of urgency to them but still gentle. *"The nerve!"* She thought but found she could not hold on to that indignation, then more rhythmic pressure on her chest, the lips, the chest.

From her seat of observation, she thought, *"Should I be alarmed at this? It is of no consequence,"* when it suddenly felt that her lungs were exploding because in fact they kind of were. There was a great streak of pain as the water her murky dream had deposited in her lungs rushed through her throat in a violent wave. She had hardly recovered by any sense as her lungs rasped in a ragged cache of clean, dry air that felt foreign to the waterlogged lungs.

"Can you hear me?" she heard. "Are you alright? Can you hear me, miss?"

"Yes, a male voice. Was that the man with… was it a man? Something silly and white." She tried to make sense of everything; what was, and what now seemed to be, did not fit. She turned her head to try and focus on the pleading voice and finally saw the boy, his eyes wide and filled with tears, a look of great relief on his face. It was a kind face.

5

SHE ASSESSED HIM to be a peasant. What was he doing?

He looked so concerned and sincere.

Her head was throbbing horribly.

"Hello miss, can you hear me? My name is Kyle, can you hear me? It's alright, you're safe now. That's right. There you are, it's alright, just breathe."

She saw his face above her, cradling her head in his arm. *What a lovely young man*, she thought. His hair was kind of shaggy around his ears; of course, it was wet and looked like they might be a sandy blonde were it dry. She would guess him to be around eighteen or so, but that is hard to judge on some people. His face was kind, she thought, with an easy smile across it. She knew she was safe as he said, safe from what she wasn't sure about, but she couldn't doubt him at that moment.

Attempting to sit up too quickly, feeling propriety insisted she removes herself from this handsome boy's arms, with that smile, and those eyes… she found herself right back where she started; Kyle had to catch her as she swooned. She was dizzy, and everything had gone all spinny.

"It's okay. I'll help you sit up. Don't move too quickly now, that's right, I've got you." He urged reassuringly. "Just try and breathe easy. Do you know your name?"

Her name? Well yes, of course, her name. She searched around her for the first time, taking in her surroundings, thinking as she did so, that surely her name wasn't a hard question. She observed they were sitting on a small beach, an inlet. Behind the boy, Kyle, yes, Kyle, and to her left were a couple of docks, with small boats moored. Along each of the docks up on the shore stood what looked like a good-sized boathouse or storage, fishing nets hanging on the sides. The sun was low in the sky to the right of and behind her, not too many paces, grew a healthy forest through which you could see well-used trails of differing sizes, some large enough for a couple of horses and carriages. On either side of her beyond the sandy shoreline stood some houses, built of shimmery wood, turned grey through time and wind and sea.

Sea… yes, the sea, she had come from the sea. Kyle had pulled her from the sea! She was drowning! Kyle saved her from drowning! Kyle… her name, he asked her name… she searched the water as if to find her name still floating there. She spotted, on the side of one of the little boats moored at the dock, painted roughly in simple white lettering, a name. Feeling foolish now and not wanting to appear daft, she answered, "Claire. My name is Claire." This was all the answer she could give.

Wide-eyed and drop-jawed, Kyle could just stare for a split second before blinking and composing himself. Suddenly self-conscious, Claire began to check herself, becoming very aware of her physicality. It was then that she noticed as if for the first time, that she was soaked to the bone and just as chilled. She was shaking uncontrollably and her teeth began to chatter.

"You need to get dry and warm. Easy now, I'll help you up, that's right, just lean on me. There you go. Let me do the work, that's good." Kyle consoled, helping Claire to her feet, his arms around her waist, pulled tightly into his side.

This uninvited intimacy felt foreign to her somehow. Her instinct was to insist he unhand her immediately, but she found she could not voice it. She was too weak and unsure. Her head really was throbbing. Her throat felt raw, and she couldn't remember ever feeling this feeble.

He was a bit too tall for her to reach his shoulder so she clung to his waist, gripping his shirt for dear life. Kyle had to mostly carry her as they headed towards one of the forest's smaller trails. She could feel the sand on her bare feet turn to small stones then to dirt, but then everything went spinny again, her knees wobbled then betrayed her completely. She felt herself being lifted gently, like a child. There was no internal protest. At last, she slept.

It was good to sleep.

6

OH, SHE WAS COMFORTABLE, so warm and comfortable, the amber sun filtering through the window's lace curtain and onto her face. Stirring reluctantly, she felt the soreness reminding her of the struggle before. She was very thirsty, her throat rough and dry. Coming out of her sleepiness, she looked around, seeing nothing familiar. Remembrance slowly came back to her as her mind awoke, the water, the sun, the sand, Kyle.

She found herself in a lovely small space, in a small soft bed. The whole room was simple but elegant in its simplicity. The pillow was made of down feathers and covered in a soft white case with delicately embroidered blue flowers on the edge. That beautiful embroidery… had she seen that before? It seemed familiar to her, but she couldn't place it. The hand-sewn quilt that covered the bed was quaint, the stitches slightly irregular but well placed. There was a small graceful table at the right of the bed, just below a window covered with a creamy lace curtain, letting in heavenly rays of warm sunlight. The sun bathed the room in an amber glow, alighting all the natural dust that floated in the air, usually unnoticed by the naked eye, were it not for the tattletale sunbeams that caught them dancing. Even more delightful was the large pitcher of water and full glass beside it, still cold and fresh with condensation pilling on the outside. It had been recently poured. She drank it gratefully as if it were the finest tea from anywhere across the sea, then poured herself another, and then she drank another.

She grasped the idea that she was no longer in the light, wet garment she had been in the last time she remembered. Pulling back the covers to discover she was now dressed in what was unmistakably a nightgown, soft as the pillowcase, made in the same fabric with the same little flowers embroidered around the collar and long sleeves. At this, she began to feel a note of panic. The only person she had seen so far was Kyle. She hadn't even seen anybody at the inlet, come to think of it. More panic set in.

Just as she spied what she thought must be her clothing hanging on the back of the door, unfamiliar but dry and clean, she heard a soft knock and the door opened slowly and ever so slightly.

"Claire, it's Kyle," he whispered, "you awake? May I come in?" and he tentatively peeked his head around the door. All she could do was nod, suddenly becoming very uncomfortable, pulling her knees to her chest and pulling the quilt up below her chin. Just as she could feel her face turning red at the thought of Kyle getting her out of her wet clothes and into this nightgown, a woman with Kyle's kind face and sandy blonde hair stepped gently in behind him. Kyle stepped aside to let the woman into the room. He then introduced her, still in his whispered tone,

"Claire, this is my mom, Helen. She and my sister Ruth cared for you after I brought you home."

An audible sigh of relief left her lips as her face finished its journey to red. She was also strangely relieved to notice Kyle's face turn a shade of pink with his eyes cast down as he slipped back out the door. Embarrassment returned, thinking that Helen may have noticed. If Helen had noticed, she did not indicate it. She stood at the end of the bed just inside the door, for there wasn't much room between the door and the foot of the bed, wearing the same easy smile as Kyle, her hands held lightly at her apron front. Her hair piled up in a loose bun, and at the back of her head had loose strands hanging along the nape of her neck and at the temples. Sunbeams that caught the dancing dust gave her hair a magical shimmer and a twinkle in her eyes.

Helen sat gently at the foot of the bed studying the newcomer's face as Claire studied hers in return. Claire found that Helen was a handsome woman with light wrinkles around her eyes and along her forehead, the kind that formed from laughter. Her skin was clear and lightly tanned and she had a slight figure that was fit and strong. Helen tilted her head slightly to the right and asked,

"How do you feel, Claire? May I?" raising her hand to feel Claire's forehead. Again Claire nodded, not yet finding her voice. Helen placed her fingertips on Claire's neck then wrist, finally lifting her chin to look into her eyes. That twinkle in Helen's eye was natural, not put there by the sun. She checked Claire's water and smiled.

"Good, good. Are you hungry? You've been sleeping for some time, dear."

Claire had to think a moment before she realized that yes, she was hungry.

"Yes, ma'am I think I could eat a bit." Her voice was still rough and her throat was still sore.

"We'll start you with some broth then." And Helen got up from the bed and turned towards the door.

"Ma'am? Please, how long have I slept?"

"Only as long as you needed, it seems. No need to worry about that. And call me Helen, please. Ma'am is much too formal." She smiled.

Claire couldn't put her finger on the thoughts tumbling just at the back of her mind. This room was so small, these clothes, too simple, these people, their manner much too informal and intimate. She felt as though she should be and was somewhat aghast but could not put reason to these concerns. So Claire simply replied, "Yes Ma'am… I mean Helen. Thank you."

Helen brought the girl broth made of vegetable stock and soon after, applesauce. The broth was warm and delicious, soothing her throat as it slid gently down. She was indeed hungry; her stomach growled loudly both in protest and gratitude as the broth found its way to her empty belly, followed delightfully by the sweet cold applesauce.

With her body feeling improved from the meal, her eyelids became heavy. She was soon sound asleep again, dreaming of funny red fish in little white wigs, waking with a start as the sound of crashing waters against… what… crashing water… *'Goodness!'* she thought, *'I think I have to go to the bathroom.'*

Opening her eyes, Claire saw that she was still in the same small room; only the light coming through the window had changed from the bright amber of early day to the orangey-pink of sundown. Sitting up slowly, remembering the spinny feeling, she tried her strength. Gladly it was returning a bit.

She draped her legs gently over the bed side, readying herself to lift her body and walk the (thankfully) short distance to the door. She got to her feet alright, but as she attempted her first step, she toppled to the right, tipping into the table at the side of the bed, the pitcher and glass tilted back and forth, threatening to topple also. Gladly neither the glass nor the pitcher fell but they made enough noise to draw Kyle's attention, who was apparently keeping vigil outside the door. He flew in so quickly that his chair flew to the floor, making more noise than Claire did with the table. Quicker than she could focus, he was at her side with his arms around her waist. Claire's face flushed red, she quickly apologized, explaining that she only had to use the bathroom. The apology felt foreign on her tongue, like a taste she wasn't quite used to. She stiffened a bit with annoyance.

Shortly behind him came his mother and another girl, maybe a couple of years younger than Kyle. Helen ran in with a look of panic while the younger girl was harder to read, maybe concerned and curious. Again Claire embarrassed herself by yelling out,

"I just have to use the bathroom!" Annoyance quickly returned, she could not remember the taste of embarrassment either.

"Kyle, help her to the bathroom." His mother instructed.

"WHAT?" Kyle and Claire yelled together, their eyes both huge.

"Oh, sorry, long day, of course not." Helen laughed quietly, "if you only could have just seen your faces," she added more to herself, and Ruth began to giggle under her breath too.

Helen cleared her throat, "Um, well, yes Kyle, give her here then. Come along Claire, I'll help you to the bathroom."

These new tastes were becoming undesirably familiar.

Exiting the room Claire had been staying in, they entered the bright kitchen lined with graying wood cabinets. The cabinets looked to be made of the same wood used on the buildings by the docks. Most of the room lay to the right of the door. Starting at Claire's closest right was the icebox, followed by the wooden countertop that wrapped the distance of the wall; around the corner, and to the far side of the room. Here the countertop was interrupted in the center by a large double sink made of porcelain, water being supplied by a single spouted pump spigot. Above the sink cut a window that fit exactly the same amount of space as the sink with cheery red and yellow floral curtains. If one were to look closely, you would see that these were also hand embroidered like the nightgown Claire was wearing and the pillowcase she laid her head on. There were cabinets above and cabinets below, with white porcelain knobs on each. The countertops looked to be made of the same rough, graying wood as the cabinets but they were polished and smooth, either by design or use. A large table sat in front of her door at the center of the kitchen. They would have to walk around the end of it to get through, on the opposite side of the table, to the left of the sink was the cookstove, where the area was open to the living room. Not only did they use the stove to cook their meals, but it also served to heat the house. At the left end of the living room was a staircase that angled back towards the kitchen. Below the stairs was a door that led to another room. All around the house you could see cozy things. There was a large soft chair with a stack of books beside it, a long couch sagging with wear, draped with quilts, and piled with soft, embroidered pillows. The front door opened to a long porch where you could sit on a swing and look over the Harrington family's land, the same view seen from the large windows that graced the walls of the living room, covered at the top with the same creamy lace as the guest room curtains. You could see past the green field that flowed from the front to the left of the house, over the top of the trees, and out across the ocean beyond the inlet. Tonight would have been an exceptional night to watch the summer sunset, but that would all wait.

For now, they were heading out a door to the left of the guest room, out to the back porch that held the laundry tub, scrubber, and wringer, accompanied by a rack of muddy boots sitting below pegs covered with work clothes. Descending three wide steps, they landed on a gravel trail that passed an empty laundry line to a little building with a moon cut out of the door. Helen helped Claire up the little step into the outhouse, showed her where to find the lamp and matches and how to light it, and left her to her business. Claire was feeling stronger as she was up and moving. The fresh night air felt wonderful in her lungs. As she finished and stepped back out of the outhouse, she noticed the rolling green hills delicately rising behind her, as well as the cute little chicken coop and the chicken's yard off to the right of the outhouse, the chickens already nestled in for the night.

She then spotted to the left, the garden that had just been planted and was beginning to sprout. It was a peaceful place, and they seemed to be kind and generous people.

Ruth was awaiting their guests' return just inside the kitchen, where she surprised Claire with a big hug. Claire was indeed taken by surprise, and it took a moment for her to tentatively hug Ruth in return. Claire noticed that the top of Ruth's head reached just under her nose. Ruth let go and stood with her hands on Claire's shoulders, looking up at her with such tenderness in her gray eyes. Claire thought surely she saw a hint of a young woman emerging from behind that child's face. Ruth let go and bid her good night. Running towards the living room, she turned to give Claire a shy smile and disappeared up the stairs.

"Good night dear," said Helen with a squeeze on Claire's shoulder, picking up her needlework and settling into the comfy chair.

Kyle stood at the sink staring at his feet, offering Claire a quick nod as she went back to her room.

On the small side table beside the bed waiting for her, wrapped in a yellow and red embroidered napkin matching the kitchen curtains, was a thick warm piece of bread covered in butter. Her water pitcher was filled with cool fresh water. A clean nightgown, this one a delicate pink with intricate eyelet cutwork at the edges, was laid out on the end of the bed along with clean undergarments. She was so touched by this family's kindness that she could feel the ever-threatening tears just hit the surface of her tear ducts, but that is where they would always stay. Just on the edge.

She felt she really should love it here. But why did it all seem so foreign to her, and why couldn't she remember being anywhere else? With anyone else? Just her dream of funny red fish in little white wigs.

She changed into the clean gown and crawled under her covers, realizing she was thinking of the room as hers already, falling asleep to the low rumbling tones of Helen and Kyle talking.

"No mom, you go to sleep, I'll be alright out here, I can doze on the couch. I'll wake you if she needs you."

"She's a blessing Kyle. Watch over her"

A blessing? Did she hear that right or was she entering into her hazy dreams again, seems a loving woman's voice had whispered that to her in another dream she could only just remember.

Beloved blessing.

7

CLAIRE WOKE TO THE SMELL of bacon and the sound as it sizzled and splat enticingly in the pan. And what was that warm, comfortable smell that wrapped you in a hug?

Sitting up carefully, she was happy to find she was feeling quite strong and well. Tentatively she swung her legs out of the bed and gently rose to her feet, pleased with the renewed feeling of strength. With the early sun just turning white from pink sifting through the lace curtain behind her, she slowly opened the door to enter the kitchen. Ruth sat at the table just finishing her breakfast, sopping up the last of the bacon grease from her plate with her biscuit, the source of that heavenly smell. Helen was at the sink washing two plates, causing Claire to glance involuntarily around the room.

"Just us girls this morning Claire," Helen responded. "Sit and have some breakfast, and if you're up to it, we can spend some lovely girl time while the boys are away." She added with a wink which was joined by Ruth's eager grin.

The breakfast was sublime, although her appetite wasn't quite back, or so she sensed. Finished with her meal, she sat, unsure of what to do next. Claire looked from her dirty dish to

Ruth, then Helen. In return, Ruth looked at Claire's empty dish, at Claire, and then at Helen. There was that indignation Claire could not put a name to. Looking at Ruth, Helen nodded her head towards the plate and then the sink indicating that Ruth should take care of Claire's dish.

Displaying her own hint of displeasure, Ruth took Claire's dish to the sink washing it with a mumbled, "Fine for now but..." before trailing off.

"Come along dear, I'll walk you to the outhouse, I need to get some things from the shed while we're outside," suggested Helen diverting the mood that was settling in the kitchen.

Claire followed Helen to the outhouse gratefully. Helen continued to an outbuilding off the end of the back porch Claire hadn't noticed the night before. Claire finished in the outhouse and went over to investigate, eager to stretch and move her body. She could hear Helen still rummaging around in the building.

"Oh, you startled me. Could you take this for me? I have a couple more things." Helen handed Claire a cream-colored porcelain basin and pitcher, a little dusty but beautiful nonetheless, adorned with delicate pink roses painted inside the basin and on the outside of the pitcher. The basin had graceful fluted edges that mimicked the curve of the pitcher's handle. Shortly Helen came out of the shed with a box in her arms, loose hair teasing at her temple. "Alright then, this is a good start," grinning as they headed back for the house.

"Ruth dear, please rinse the basin and pitcher while I get some water warming on the stove." After which, Helen scurried off to her room under the stairs, leaving Claire there for a moment, not quite sure what to do. She didn't need to worry long, for Helen came practically dancing out of her room with a dress and some other fabric items draped over one arm and something wrapped in fabric tucked under the other arm supported with both hands.

Helen led Claire back into the guest room, deposited her armful on the bed, and then brought in the box. From inside the box, Helen produced a brush and comb set. Both were made from highly polished, carved, bone or ivory.

"These were mine for the longest time," Helen informed Claire, "but Kyle made me a set for my birthday a couple of years ago that he carved. He is a talented woodworker. Of course, those quickly became my favorite." She smiled that easy smile with such love for her son in her eyes. Claire couldn't help but smile herself. "I would love for you to have these." She added as she placed them on the dresser. "Let's see," she continued as she dug in the box, "a toothbrush; oh, the toothbrush is new dear, I like to keep a couple of extras around, can't be sure when the next ship will bring them in; and tooth powder." These went into the top dresser drawer.

At this time, Ruth brought in the basin and pitcher filled with steaming water, adding them to the dresser's top. She then made herself at home at the head of the bed, plopping unceremoniously next to Claire, causing her to fall against the side of Ruth, eliciting an internal annoyance that she schooled quickly, not knowing where the impertinent reaction stemmed from.

"Thank you, Ruth." Helen smiled. Done with the box, she turned to the pile that she had laid on the bed.

"A couple of face cloths and hand towels," she explained, putting them in the top drawer. "One more nightdress I think will do, and two more sets of undergarments. I have two pairs of warm stockings for you for now, we can get more in town, but the weather is warming up and you probably won't be wearing them much." These all went into the second drawer.

"And here," she continued tentatively, "a dress. It's a little old-fashioned but it doesn't fit me anymore. You look about my old size," at this, she sent a wink to Ruth, "before kids. Well, we will get some fabric to make you a couple more dresses and we'll buy you a new, already made one. Oh, you'll need an overcoat and a sweater in case of chilly nights."

Saying these things more to herself than to anyone there, ticking off a list in her head. "Shoes! Dear, I'll dig you up a pair before we go into town. You can't walk down there barefoot."

Claire hadn't said a word through all of this. Her mind was whirling. It was all so much and they gave so willingly. She felt that somehow she should be used to being spoiled, but this was something different, she knew. This family didn't seem to be of great means, they did not seem to want for much, but their life was still simple.

"And finally," Helen said excitedly, interrupting Claire's thoughts. "This was mine as a girl; we received a new one as a gift when we got married."

Helen then unwrapped the cloth from around a mirror bordered by a beautifully ornate carved wood frame. The mirror itself was aging and pocked, the glass giving off an amber tint. Helen put it on the stand atop the dresser.

"It's old. They make them so much clearer now. But there you go! All the things you need for a proper young woman's room."

In her mind, Claire saw the shadow of a girl and a man, who may have been the father, in an opulent room, layers of rich fabric draping tall windows. She saw artwork on the wall and a full body mirror all framed in gold. The man presented the girl with a stunning gown of velvet overlaid with multiple sheer fabrics. The father laid the gown on a large overstuffed bed adorned with a canopy of more layers of sheer fabrics, the bedding as fancy as the dress itself. The man looked expectant, awaiting the girl's approval.

Claire cleared her throat and shook off the image, not wanting to see the girl's response, afraid the man would stand disappointed. She did not want to see this. It gave her a strange sense of guilt. Finding her voice she said, "Helen, I don't know how to thank you. I feel it's more than I deserve."

In answer, Helen hugged Claire gently, kissing her forehead. "Don't you give it another thought. Come along Ruth, let's let Claire clean up and get ready for the day. Then you can show her around."

8

CLAIRE CLEANED UP, avoiding the mirror, and clothed herself in the 'new' dress. It fit surprisingly well. Perhaps it fell a little longer on her than it had on Helen, hitting her just above the ankle. The dress was styled with short cap sleeves and a slightly scooped neck. The waistline was high, hitting just below her breasts with a wide, deep blue ribbon wrapping around her torso and tying in the back. The fabric was light and flowing in the palest of blues, covered with tiny deep blue flowers that matched the ribbon.

Picking up the brush and starting through her hair and finding many knots, Claire decided she should take a look in the mirror. Taking a deep breath, she said out loud, "I don't know what you're so afraid of, might as well get it over with," scolding herself.

Standing in front of the mirror was like meeting someone for the first time. Perhaps it is better explained as that phenomenon when you meet somebody and you know that you've never met them before, but they seem so familiar, giving you that strange feeling of déjà vu. Claire discovered her hair was to the middle of her back and had a dirty-looking light auburn tone. It did look like a mess; she hadn't washed since she was brought out of the sea. The frizz could possibly turn to nice waves if washed. Her face was pretty enough, she thought; her eyes light brown with specks of darker brown splashed about. A few freckles danced across the bridge of her nose, a fact that made her giggle a little. Her mouth was full and had a serious look to it, like she was deep in thought. Perhaps there was a suggestion of a smile at the edge. Maybe the slight circles under her eyes would go away with time. She wasn't very fond of that feature. All in all, she was pleased with what she saw.

Ruth announced herself at the door just as Claire was starting to try and get the brush through her hair again, "Claire, I brought you some of my ribbons if you would like them for your hair. You don't need to use them if they are too childish for you."

"I think I like ribbons." Claire answered, then after a moment she asked, "Ruth, how old would you guess I am because I seriously have no idea."

Ruth thought for a moment and looked at Claire contemplatively, answering "I don't know. Hmmm. I'd guess around seventeen or eighteen."

Claire looked back into the mirror, pulling the hair away from her face, turning her head this way and then that. Straightening out her dress, she considered her figure, finally saying, "Yes, that's probably about right," adding after a moment, "do you think you could help me with my hair? I can't even seem to get the brush through it."

Ruth practically jumped out of her shoes (had she been wearing any) with excitement. The smile on the edge of Claire's mouth became more than a mere suggestion.

As Ruth tried to pull the brush through Claire's hair, she asked, "Would you like me to help you wash your hair? We can wash it out in the bathhouse!" And without waiting for an answer, she grabbed Claire's hand, leading her out the back door to the outbuilding Helen had retrieved the pitcher and basin from earlier.

"This is the bathhouse," Ruth explained, "Dad built it. He's very good at making things. See? He built a system under the ground so that we could drain the wash barrel and the sink. We can heat water on the stove and get the water right here, from the sink! We don't have to haul it from the outside well like some people. But there isn't any water heated yet today, do you mind cold water?" Ruth asked without actually waiting for an answer. "All the soaps and towels are in the cupboard here."

Ruth continued to tell Claire all about the bathhouse and her father's cleverness. There was a small potbelly stove at the back of the room to heat the water and the room simultaneously. The trick was to make the first couple pans of water super hot and as you got to the last ones, the first ones you poured in the barrel cooled down enough that the water was perfect. When you were done bathing, you pulled the plug from the bottom of the barrel and the water ran down a pipe into the ground where it filtered through gravel, then rocks and finally the dirt. Their dad used the same system for the sink in the kitchen.

"What made my dad so smart about all of this is he had to figure out the drainage before he built everything else! He's super smart that way," she added with pride.

With Claire's hair washed and combed through, the girls decided to let it dry before adding the ribbon. Claire decided to get a look at her hair now that it was clean, and yes, it was a light auburn tone that was very pretty, with a soft wave to it.

Claire and Ruth donned aprons and went to find Helen and see what she would like them to do. There were always chores to be done. Helen was feeding the chickens, and when the girls arrived, she handed them a basket to go gather eggs.

"If you feed the chickens first," Ruth informed Claire, "they are busy so they don't peck at you when you try and take their eggs! Chickens can be pretty cheeky creatures."

Cheeky indeed! Claire wasn't so sure she liked these chickens with the squawking and pecking. Most of them pecked away, content at the scratch that Helen had thrown. Sir Rooster, however, decided it was his job to show this newcomer with new smells who was the boss of the coop. He chased poor Claire right out of the laying pen, and it was all she could do not to drop the eggs she had resting in her apron while escaping with what she was sure was her very life. She came out of it unscathed but the eggs did not. The contents of the eggs were sliding down the front of her apron as Helen and Ruth laughed helplessly.

Clumsily exiting the pen, Claire was met by the curious gander having heard the commotion. He took it upon himself to finish what the rooster had started and make sure this newcomer was convinced of her place within the pecking order. Helen recovered a stick and shooed the goose away. Poor Claire was not at all a fan of this feeling of disrespect the feathered creatures had shown her. She was even less fond of the laughter at her expense and stood there feeling quite cross.

Seeing Claire's discomfort, Helen put her arm around Claire's shoulder and reassured her. "Come now Claire, it's all right. Not too bad for your first time out. Shake yourself off now, you'll get the hang of it and the chickens will get used to you too."

After tending chickens, and an apron change, all three of the ladies went down to the barn, where they taught Claire how to milk the goat and cow. They got a little later start than usual today so Minnie, the goat, was not happy. Rose, the cow, was also quite uncomfortable but didn't show her displeasure as openly as Minnie. She was just thankful to be relieved of her morning supply.

Milking went a little better for Claire after a couple of tries at the teats. She found the milking rhythm soothing compared to the intrusion of gathering eggs. Encircling the top of the teat between thumb and forefinger and then gently rolling each finger along its length reminded her of playing an instrument.

There it was again, an echo of something.

From below the barn where the property slanted down a slight, steady hill, galloped the family's mare, Sunrise. Sunrise was a beautiful bay about fourteen hands high, a sweet girl, sturdy and hardworking with a laid back and funny personality, usually. As with the goat, she noticed that the ladies of the house were running late this morning and she was keen for her oats and grooming. She nudged Claire playfully, but a little harder than necessary, seeing what she could get away with towards this newcomer. Claire felt quite impatient with having to gain these animals' approval and Sunrise picked up on her ire. Ruth was able to brush Sunrise, talk to her and settle her down. "You know Claire, these creatures are quite clever and can feel when you are not right within yourself. Come here and meet Sunrise properly. Put your hand here to her nose. Make a soft fist and let her smell you." Claire timidly did as she was instructed. At first, Sunrise sneezed, startling Claire, who pulled away quickly.

"Try again," Ruth extended.

Claire put her fist up for the mare to inspect once more, and both Sunrise and Claire relaxed as Ruth reassured them both, speaking just as gently to Claire as she did the mare. Helen watched as Sunrise and Claire both relaxed and Claire slowly began to pet Sunrise along her neck. Sunrise nudged Claire again, only gently this time. Ruth was thrilled and took Claire over to snuggle the goat and cow now that they were all fed and comfortable.

"I'd swear the milk tastes sweeter after Ruth has a talk with Minnie." Helen teased.

After the animals were tended to, they went to the garden, weeded out any new weeds, and laid out the watering grid. This was also one of the things that their dad had made. It was an ingenious grid of tubes, made of oilcloth that Helen sewed together, that attached to the garden's water pump spigot. Just below the spigot was a bladder they would fill and the water would trickle down to seep out along the rows. The family would fill the bladder anywhere from two to four times a day, depending on the weather and how far along the plant's growth was.

After finishing the outside chores for the afternoon, the women went inside to start dinner. In the evening when all the nightly chores were done, they would have a simple supper. Dinner was usually the largest meal of the day. Helen had already started a chicken cooking for soup that morning. As it was the beginning of planting season and there weren't a lot of fresh vegetables for the broth, they used stock that Helen had canned at harvest last season, vegetables they had dried, and what was almost the end of the potatoes that they stored in a root cellar under the back porch. Claire was amazed at all the clever surprises she was finding around the property. Everything had a double duty, it seemed. She hadn't even noticed that the 'table' she thought she had seen the laundry tub, scrubber, and wringer on was also an entrance to the root cellar where the family kept their canned goods, roots, dried meats, and fruits. The root cellar walls were all large rocks and mortar with shelves and herbs hung from the low ceiling. There was goat cheese curing on a set of shelves against the back wall. So much of this family's daily routine was unfamiliar to Claire. But why? Had she just forgotten or had she never known? The more she learned, the more she realized she didn't know.

Helen took a collection of small tins from the cupboard nearest the stove and handed them to Claire. "What do you think the soup needs?" Helen asked Claire encouragingly.

"I, I don't know. I don't know if I know," Claire responded nervously.

Helen instructed, "Stir the soup like this and take a good smell. It helps if you breathe in through your mouth a little too.

Now, trust your instincts and smell the herbs, one at a time and see if they smell right, then add a small palm full."

Reluctantly, Claire did as she was taught and found that she could 'taste' as she breathed in the aromas of the soup and the herbs what herbs were needed. She was very pleased with herself as Helen reassured her and praised her efforts, feeling that perhaps this was the first thing she had ever done on her own or the first time anyone ever expected her to be able to do something on her own.

As the soup was simmering, Helen taught Claire to make bread dough. They would get the dough going tonight and bake it early in the morning. The hotter the days got, the earlier the bread was baked. Claire discovered that she loved to make and knead dough. She loved the smell of the yeast, along with the simmering soup and herbs.

Kyle came walking up the trail that led from town to home just as they were finishing up the last of the bread. He went directly to the barn where he took off his shirt, dumped his head under the water spout, and proceeded to wash off a hard morning's work, unloading cargo from the ships that returned today. Ruth had run upstairs and met him at the front door with a clean shirt.

"Thanks, Ruthie," Kyle said with that easy grin. "Wow Mom, that soup smells like you outdid yourself. It had my stomach growling halfway up from the barn."

"Claire seasoned it up today," Helen answered with obvious pride as she tilted her head towards Claire, who was cutting thick slices of yesterday's bread.

Kyle saw Claire for the first time that day, and his mouth dropped open a moment before he could stop himself. "Claire, you look great!" He stammered; again before he could stop himself.

With the flush of fresh air and honest work on her cheeks, her hair washed and pulled back loosely in one of Ruth's ribbons now, she did look beautiful. Of course, Kyle couldn't help but notice how nicely Claire's borrowed dress flattered her figure.

"Thank you" was all she could whisper. This of course caused a grin on both Ruth and Helen's faces, not helping either Kyle or Claire feel any better.

"Soup's on!" announced Helen breaking the awkward silence. They all set to getting bowls and butter, soup and spoons and sat at the large kitchen table. Helen sat at the head of the table at the sink end, Kyle in a chair on one side and Ruth and Claire on the other.

"I talked to one of the Captains that came in today. You remember Captain Thomas, right Mom?" Kyle announced,

"He told me he saw Dad at his last stop just about three weeks out. So dad should be coming home soon. Said he had a really good load too. This trip should pay off the rest of what's owed on the ship, and then what we get from the harvest this fall, Dad shouldn't have to go to sea at all next winter."

"That is really good news, dear. This was a long trip, but it sounds like it was all worth it." Helen returned, her eyes wet with the start of tears.

At Claire's look of confusion and concern, Helen explained, "My husband Robert is the Captain of the ship Helena – isn't that sweet – where he earns his living as a sea merchant. He travels across the sea to many foreign lands, buying or trading goods. On his return, he sells the things he's brought back to the people here or to those that come across the land to this port to buy supplies. The local shops buy quite a bit of the items, but most merchandise goes to cities and townships inland that don't have ports of their own and will come here to buy and trade. The summer and harvest times are very busy. Local farmers grow apples and wheat, straw, and hay of all kinds as well as produce, like us, or grow chickens, harvest eggs, and have cattle. We make cheese from our goat's milk and make and can butter from the cow. Not only is our Ruth good with the animals, but she also has an amazing green thumb. She has some berries that she tends over the hill at the far side of the property that produces so much that there is no way we can use them all. We make jellies for our own use and sell some at the summer market. People come from quite a distance to buy baskets of her berries." At this, Ruth sat up even straighter and beamed a giant smile, "They are the largest and sweetest around. Kyle makes beautiful brush and comb sets, for people and animals. Robert imports camel and boar hair for them. Kyle also makes jewelry boxes and all kinds of little boxes. They're just beautiful, wait until you see them." At this, Kyle moaned and sank deeper into his chair. "I do needlework and sew if you haven't noticed it," she grinned, "My nightgowns are quite sought after, thankfully."

9

AND SO THE next few weeks went, Helen taught Claire how to stoke the fire just right so as not to bake the bread too fast and how to test when it's done by thumping lightly on the bottom. The women took care of the animals in the morning. Did the milking, groomed the horse, and tended the garden. They baked bread and made more soups from canned venison and rabbit.

On the days that there weren't any ships to unload or merchandise to shuffle within the storages or to the stores, Kyle would set traps for rabbits or bow hunt for deer. Not surprisingly, he made his own arrows. In the evenings while the women were getting supper ready, Kyle would tend to the animals and fill the garden's watering bladder one last time if needed. The evening would usually wind down out on the porch watching the sunset and listening to the night sounds, or they would all sit around the table and play a game of cards. One of their favorites was called 'spite malice', but it was all in good fun. Kyle would sometimes sit on the front porch and carve on his latest project. Ruth was trying to learn how to do needlework, although she didn't quite have the love for it as her mom. Helen was teaching Claire how to do clothing repairs and had her help in some of her sewing. Claire was getting stronger every day, enjoying the rewards of hard work and learning new things; that sense of accomplishment only good honest work could bring.

One particular evening after a couple of days of the chickens refusing to lay eggs, Kyle set out a live trap behind the chicken coop. He was sure he had seen a fox lurking the night before as he was tending the chickens for the evening. The next morning his suspicions were confirmed. There in the trap was a terrified little red fox. Ruth took pity on the scared little creature and convinced her mom and Kyle to let her try and reason with it. She spent some time with the caged fox explaining that if she didn't leave the chickens alone she would be unable to convince her brother not to track her down and make a lovely muff out of her. It seemed to work. The chickens started laying eggs again. When Claire asked Ruth how she did it, she just told her that some animals are easier to reason with than others.

"That's not what I mean, Ruthie," Claire had picked up Kyle's nickname for Ruth, "you actually seem to be able to *talk* to the animals!"

"Oh, I wouldn't say I actually 'talk' to them. We just understand each other. Dad says it's my other talent. He says we have earthly talents and other talents. Sometimes I just feel what they feel. It works with people too sometimes," she gave Claire an impish grin that Claire wasn't quite sure how to take.

About two weeks before Robert was due to return, Helen planned a trip into town with Claire and Ruth. Helen found an old pair of shoes for Claire to wear. Claire had adopted Ruth's habit of going barefoot around the farm, and they had yet to traverse off the homestead.

"These are my old ones dear; they'll get you into town anyway, we'll get you a proper pair when we're there." Helen apologized.

The shoes were made of the softest tawny leather with gentle creases worn across the toe. They looked like a slipper and felt just as comfortable, but the sole was sturdy. They fit just a little big and took the shape of what must have been Helen's foot, but they would be wonderful to walk in for the dirt road turned into small stones than sand towards town. She felt they were maybe the most comfortable shoes she had ever worn.

Ruth grabbed half a dozen rounds of cheese from the root cellar. Helen carried a basket containing four dozen eggs, handing Claire three large empty bags to carry items home in. Claire's stomach was filled with butterflies as they headed down the hill towards town. The only time she had been in town was when Kyle hauled her out of the sea, which was a blur of thought and image. As far as she could remember, the Harrington family, apart from Robert, were the only people she could remember ever knowing. Besides the fuzzy visions of a certain man, woman, and young woman, whom she was not at all sure she liked; she could not find another face. She didn't even see anybody on the day of her 'arrival'. Aside from the butterflies, Claire was eager to see this town and do some shopping. It all felt exhilarating.

The walk to town took about thirty minutes, down and around the hill. They passed two smaller homes towards town, one yellow, the other a pale blue. Next, a taller two-story home, painted white, just as the woods opened to the inlet. To their left sat the church that doubled as the schoolhouse, and they also saw the big feed and seed building. They walked to their right on the pebble/sandy road leading past the docks and into the center of town. Boardwalks ran along the front of buildings, starting and ending in steps at the side alleys. Some buildings had porch-like covers extending over the boardwalk with benches sitting here and there. All the windows of the shops were flanked with shutters of different designs and colors.

The town consisted of a post office, a bakery restaurant, a hotel, and the general store that carried groceries and assorted sundries; this is where Helen bought her fabric, sewing, and needlework supplies. They passed a few people coming out of the bakery or the post office. They nodded friendly greetings giving Claire curious glances. Residents here were kind and used to strangers since it was a port town, but had heard of the girl staying with the Harrington's and were naturally interested.

At the general store, Helen picked out two pretty calico fabrics after fussing over many of them, asking Claire and Ruth which were their favorites, changing her mind then repeating the process; twice. When she went to pay, she traded the eggs and cheese for the purchase and received a little coin on top of it. She and the grocer talked about the weather, the fox, and the latest deliveries. After introducing Claire to the grocer named Mr. Hansen and explaining simply that Claire was a friend of the family and that they were out getting her some new things, Mr. Hansen told Helen about the nice shipment of women's clothing that had just come in; so that is where they headed to next.

On the opposite side of the street facing the ocean was a huge and very important-looking two-story building. A deck ran all along the upper level with lounge chairs overlooking the town, the storage buildings, and out across the inlet. This building was book-ended by a tavern and a mortuary. This important-looking building Claire could see by the impressive sign hanging off the upper deck was the town's bank and import-export business. It gave her an unsolicited chill, but then she noticed that Helen and Ruth must have shared her distaste because they were also looking at it with wrinkled noses.

"Come on girls. This is where we want to go." Helen caught her grimace, replaced it with a smile, and led them into the clothing store.

There was truly quite a new selection, according to Helen and Ruth. They examined the new items excitedly, accompanied by many oohs and ahhs. Claire rummaged through a few items, finding a couple of dresses she liked, but wasn't quite as enthusiastic about it as Ruth and Helen, leaving everything on the racks instead of gathering an armful to try on like the other two.

"Let's go try some things on, come on Claire," Helen urged, and as they got to the dressing rooms, she handed Claire the dresses instead of going in herself. "Ruth, you take that room, and Claire you can take that one, I think these will be your size. Pick your favorites, but I want to see you in them! I'll be right back."

The girls tried on probably five dresses, each coming out to show each other, each turning this way and that, checking the fit in the standing full-length mirror.

Contemplating the third dress, a sweet light blue piece with a small matching ribbon tied around the waist, Claire found herself drawn into another vision or memory. In the mirror stood a young girl of Claire's age and stature, happy in her new light blue dress, swishing the many layers of fabric back and forth while a second young lady was trying to tuck the ends of matching ribbon into plaits at the back of the swishing girl's hair. Claire could see that this second girl was dressed noticeably less refined and trying to hide her frustration with the girl in blue. Returning to the present, she saw Ruth behind her in the mirror, looking at her inquisitively. Claire smiled sheepishly, removing the dress deciding not to take that one before Ruth or Helen could even offer an opinion.

By the time they were done, Ruth and Claire each had a new dress in their bag. Claire also left feeling a little guilty with a new pair of shoes much like her borrowed ones and a charming sweater.

"It's too much Helen; I need to figure out a way to earn my way if I'm to stay around here." Claire protested.

"You already do, dear, don't you worry about that now. And you never can tell what you may accomplish when the opportunity presents itself. Please Claire; really, don't give it another thought. I'm happy to do this for you. It makes me happy." Helen assured her.

They had just left the store and started down the boardwalk when a man began to approach them. Claire thought sure she heard a small groan come from Helen and saw Ruth pull back slightly behind her mother. The man approached, walking with a posture of superiority. Claire was immediately repulsed by this man but not so much by his appearance but by his attitude, although his appearance wasn't all that pleasant either. He wasn't that much taller than Claire, his hair was full and white with age which would normally be considered a good attribute, but he wore it in an odd high upsweep on the top of his head. The hairstyle could almost be measured as feminine. He wore a very stiff suit that anyone could tell was expensive. He had a red handkerchief folded to look like a fishtail tucked into his breast pocket. The suit bellowed out below his well-fed belly and cast a shadow on his very shiny shoes. His face was round and powder pale with a red flush around his eyes and nose.

"Good day Mrs. Harrington, out doing some shopping, are you?" he greeted with a counterfeit air of affability, turning his attention obviously to Claire. "Good day, Mr. Orson. May I introduce a friend of the family? This is Claire. Claire, this is Mr. Orson, the owner of the bank." Helen responded, missing her usual genuineness indicating the large bank with a nod of her head. To which Ruth added in a quiet grumble behind Helen "And most of the town."

"Claire is staying with us for a while." Helen finished, swooshing Ruth discreetly behind her back.

"Lovely." Mr. Orson replied in a not-so-pleasant tone that made Claire's skin crawl. "Staying with the Harrington's, are you? They have the best piece of property in this whole province I'd say." He sneered with a meaningful look towards Helen and added, "My very generous offer still stands Helen, when will you convince that husband of yours to sell it to me.

It really is too much for you and your children to care for with him away so much. It really would be better for you to buy a nicer home on a smaller piece of land, maybe closer to town."

"I appreciate your concern Mr. Orson, but I support my husband's decision. And we manage just fine. But thank you. Now, we really must go. Nice to see you again, have a lovely afternoon sir." Helen's retort was cold.

"We'll see, Mrs. Harrington. I like to own the best and your property is the best. I'm used to getting what I want," he said with a barely hidden tone of a threat, his eyes cold and looking defiantly at Helen. Then quickly, his expression changed to what was supposed to be cordial, turning to Claire, saying, "It was most lovely meeting you, Claire." He bowed and walked past them deliberately close.

"I just don't like him, mom! His concern has nothing to do with us. He's just a greedy fat man!" Ruth fumed.

"Ruth! That is no way to speak about anybody. I agree that his motives are purely selfish, but it does not excuse your disrespect. Your father still needs to do business with him so keep your peace." Helen continued, "He will not get our land."

"How can you be so sure, he's bought out and driven away too many families already. He won't stop until he owns the whole county. Just because he is the only bank around he thinks he owns everybody," Ruth complained.

"Never mind him now. Your dad isn't worried about it so neither am I. Come on, no more about it. Let's get home. How are your berries doing? Is there enough for a pie? How would you like to learn to bake a pie, Claire?"

<h1 style="text-align:center">10</h1>

KYLE WAS JUST SECURING his boat to the dock when he saw his mom, sister, and Claire walking out of town towards home. He waved his arms and shouted for their attention, running up to them with a large fish in his possession.

"Hey mom!" he exclaimed, "I've caught dinner!"

"Excellent Kyle, are you done here? Walk home with us?" his mom inquired.

"Absolutely. Claire, you've got new shoes," Kyle noticed. "They're nice." He grinned and Claire blushed then Kyle quickly added, "What did you get, Ruth?"

Ruth talked excitedly about their shopping trip, not leaving out a single detail and barely taking a breath all the way home. She told him how beautiful Claire looked in all the dresses and how hard it was to pick just one. "And we got you a new summer work shirt, by the way" she squeezed in. She told Kyle all about the encounter with Mr. Orson with quite a bit of personal commentary, which received a quick scolding from Mom.

"That Mr. Orson is getting more aggressive about our property, Mom. I sure hope that we are able to pay off the

Helena with the money and goods dad brings on this trip and get out from underneath that man. I just cringe every time he tries to talk to me," Kyle hissed. "He has more than enough for his own needs Mom, why does he think he needs *our* land too? And what gets me is that he feels he is *entitled* to it."

"Ok, this is my theory kids," Helen explained, "even with all his possessions, all his best and beautiful things, his *large* important bank building and import-export business, he is still lonely. He tries to fill his life with things. He believes that he is serving his community by the way he runs his business, but that is just a business. He doesn't truly ever serve the people. He runs his business for profit, which is alright. We all need to make a living, but he keeps his surplus, and he doesn't give back. That is an empty existence if you ask me. I'm sure somewhere he has gifts and talents, but he keeps them hidden away to serve his own purposes or maybe out of fear. I don't know his motives and probably he doesn't either. Now, we're almost home, let's put this matter behind us. We've given Mr. Orson enough of our energy today. Kyle, you clean that fish for me and you girls go get some berries after we get these bags in the house and we'll have a delicious fish dinner and berry pie tonight!"

And that is what they did. Claire learned to make pie and she added a 'secret' ingredient that Helen had never thought of before and it turned out heavenly.

A few more days had passed and Claire was falling into a comfortable routine. She and Kyle were developing an easy attraction to each other. Kyle was quick to notice Claire's little triumphs, the new things she was learning and mastering, like the new dress she helped make from the fabric Helen purchased. She loved the way he laughed so easily and worked so hard but never forgot to play. He was so gentle and patient with his sister; respectful and caring with his mother. He never showed resentment towards the absence of his father and the extra responsibility that was put on him. Ruth was so full of energy all the time, sometimes all Claire could do was watch her and laugh to herself, Ruth was a whirlwind. And Helen, always patient and encouraging in teaching Claire new things, so talented and beautiful with the dignity that came with her years. Claire sensed wisdom within Helen that she could only hope to someday understand or even own a portion of. She trusted this family but was still haunted by the feeling that she was supposed to be somewhere else, that this wasn't the life she was meant to live. This was the life she wanted but couldn't yet give herself over to. There were too many unanswered questions way back in her head that she couldn't unravel enough to even start to make sense of.

Kyle received word that their father should be returning home within the week. Helen decided to make another trip into town, taking the horse and the family's small wagon. She instructed Kyle and Ruth to buy some chicken feed and a bag of oats from the feed and seed and take the wagon back home; she and Claire would walk home when they were done with their errands.

Helen and Claire sold the eggs and cheese they had brought to the general store's owner and then took the money to deposit at the bank. Much to Helen's distaste, Mr. Orson was there and noticed them before they could slip out. Before they could get to the door, he slipped in front of them, eyes on Claire the whole time, for she was the newest beautiful thing in town.

"Good day Mrs. Harrington," he said as he took Claire's hand and bent to kiss it, "Claire, it is a pleasure to see you are still in town. I would love to show you my collection of finery." He insisted, leading her by the elbow towards the stairs leading to the second level, "Of course, you will come along Helen that would only be proper. Coming?" he asked as if they had a choice.

Claire glanced over at Helen helplessly. Helen rolled her eyes, shrugged her shoulders, and indicated with her hand to go ahead and took up steps behind them up the stairs. Mr. Orson continued to lead Claire by the elbow with a tighter grip than necessary as if Claire would flee. The funny thing is, that is exactly what Claire felt like doing, but she knew that would be a mistake, and she chose to be polite to this man. It wasn't only about what she wanted at that moment. She fought her urge to react impetuously and, pulling her arm haughtily out of his grip, instead, she chose to take the tour graciously, not wanting to be the cause of unnecessary tension between the Harrington family and Mr. Orson.

As they entered the door at the top of the stairs Mr. Orson yelled abruptly and quite vocally, startling Claire, "OLIVIA! TEA FOR THREE IN THE LIBRARY!" then explained dismissively, "my housemaid."

He then proceeded to lead them down a hall covered in paintings, explaining along the way about each, how he got it, who the artist was and how important the artist was. This all would have been very interesting and enjoyable because he did have an eye for great art and value, had he not been completely focused on how much each piece cost him and to what great lengths he went to acquire them. They passed a great dining room furnished with a large table that could seat twelve. The furniture was made of dark, highly polished wood with elaborately carved legwork, with chairs of matching wood covered in velvety high cushions. Above the table hung a great crystal chandelier that held nearly two dozen candles.

Finally, they came to the library at the end of a long hall, passing doors leading to extra rooms, they assumed. Claire thought this was a lot of house for one man and in passing, that the bank didn't seem as big downstairs to house all this upstairs. The library was wall-to-wall shelves filled with books with breaks in the shelving to frame more art and collectibles. Mr. Orson finally let go of Claire's elbow, having reached his final destination. As Olivia entered with the tea, leaving it on a small table between two wing-back chairs in front of a bay window, Mr. Orson directed Claire and Helen's attention to one particular shelf.

"This is my prized possession," he puffed. "It can be dated back over one hundred years. I've had it analyzed by half a dozen art restorers and historians at great expense."

Claire's head started to get that familiar spinny feeling as she came closer to see an exquisite woman's shoe. It was a lovely light blue velvet with ethereal hand-embroidered flowers in multiple shades of blue and lavender. Crystal beadwork and small gems were elegantly worked into the design. The shoe boasted a bit of heel, the type that would be worn by a girl who was now considered to be a young woman. Claire's knees buckled, and Helen was at her side in an instant.

"Is she ill? What is the matter with her?" asked Mr. Orson, more annoyed than concerned.

"Perhaps we've done too much today," Helen explained weekly, "May we sit a moment?"

"Of course, of course. Olivia, pour the girl her tea," was Mr. Orson's gruff response.

Helen and Claire made their way quietly to the dock where Kyle kept his small boat. They sat with their shoes off, toes dangling just in the water. After sitting for some time looking off into the far-off sea Helen asked, "What is on your mind, Claire? Care to talk about what happened back there?"

"I don't want to sound crazy. But it all seems too crazy," Claire confided.

"Give me a try" Helen returned with a nudge of her shoulder.

"Ok," Claire began. "Do you believe in past lives?"

Helen thought for a moment then answered, "Well, I don't know if I do or not. I don't *not* believe, if that makes any sense. Why?"

"It's just, I feel like, I don't know." Claire took a deep breath "Ok, I couldn't have just come out of nowhere, a gift from the sea,s" Claire chuckled weakly. "And I have these dreams and visions. They aren't all that clear but sometimes they feel so real. I see a girl and I feel like it's me, but it doesn't look like me and I, I don't like her. I don't want to be her. There are people, maybe my parents, but something bad happens to them and it's my fault or that girl's fault. They're dead. I'm sure they're dead. I can see it! Pirates or sailors and shouting; barrels, their feet going over their head just before they fly over the side! Then there's this man, I don't like him, I can't ever see him clearly, shouting orders. And there are these silly red fish, always these silly red fish in white wigs. All I know is I don't want it to be real. Then there was that shoe.

I've seen that shoe before. But how could I have? It's over one hundred years old! It's all too crazy Helen, and I don't know what to make of any of it. What if I'm not what I think I am? I mean, I don't even know what or who it *is* that I think I am."

Helen just looked at Claire for a moment before attempting to answer. "Well, I'm not sure I have an answer for you Claire, but first, let's look at this practically. The thing that has been puzzling me since Kyle found you is this; there hadn't been any reports of anybody going missing off a ship nearby. And it would have had to be nearby, or you would never have made it. Robert and the other captains of the ships that travel through this area work together for the welfare of the trading business. They look out for each other. They leave news at ports and there are groups at the shore that would have been alarmed had there been any trouble and anybody with a boat available would go help. Kyle is a volunteer. See these other vessels? All these men are rescue volunteers. The men with bigger vessels carry more crew and go out further and such. But nothing was reported. We had just had a ship in that morning. When Kyle finished helping unload, he had been out fishing. And pirates?" Helen chuckled, "There haven't been problems with pirates for a very long time. That is one of the side effects of cooperation between captains."

Helen paused for a moment looking out to the sea, gathering her thoughts. "I'm not saying that it is impossible,"

Helen continued, "but it seems unlikely that you are remembering actual events. But it does leave a lot unexplained and I wish I had an answer for you there. But I will tell you this Claire." With this she turned to look Claire directly in the eyes, her hand resting on her knee, "We all have things in our past that we wish we could change, but we can't undo what's been done. We can only move forward. Whatever this girl represents to you, learn from it. You must puzzle this one out for yourself. Know that I believe you are here for a reason. It's up to you to figure it out. Don't look backward too much, Claire. All we can do is learn, let go and move forward."

Claire just nodded, and the women embraced. The sky was turning pink; they put on their shoes and started in comfortable silence for home.

11

KYLE HADN'T BEEN gone long this morning. The women were just finishing up the morning chores when he came running up the path towards home at a dead run, shrieking, "Dad is back! Dad is back!"

As quickly as they could, the family hitched the horse to the small wagon and started toward town. The church bells rang as they got closer to their reunion. Many families were gathering at the shore to welcome the ship and its crew. Although the port saw many ships come and go, this one was coming home. Not only was Robert from this town, but the majority of his crew was too. If not in this town, then they lived in one of the neighboring villages or cities further inland. Children were running along the beach, jumping up and down and waving their little arms around, trying to get their father's first attention. Women were wiping back tears as they stood anxiously waiting to welcome home husbands, brothers, and sons. The crew was hanging over the side of the ship, waving as enthusiastically as the children. They were just as anxious to be in the arms of their families, hear the stories of how things had been while they were away, and nervous to see how much their children had grown, and if they would still know their fathers.

Claire stood behind the Harrington women, unsure of what to do. Kyle had gone to the dock to help bring in the ship. Claire was feeling very nervous and out of place. As the men started coming ashore and scanning the crowd for their families, more squeals filled the air, and even more tears of joy started flowing.

Claire's stomach was turning inside out. "Maybe I should wait for you at home. I feel like I'm intruding," she suggested.

"Nonsense, you stay right here with us. Robert will be wanting to…I want Robert to meet you right away! He'll love you. Don't worry." Helen assured Claire as she pulled her lovingly by the arm to her side. "He'll be the last to leave the ship I'm sure, he always lets his crew go first."

And he was. He grabbed Kyle once he got to the dock in a long, sincere embrace as if to never let go. Kyle was nearly as tall as his father. Robert pushed him away by the shoulders to get a look at him and pulled him back into an embrace as if he couldn't believe it was Kyle. They walked with their arms around each other's shoulders, talking excitedly until they reached the end of the dock where the women had moved to greet them. Robert dropped his bag and ran to the rest of his family. Ruth practically flew into his arms and buried her head into his shoulder, sobbing joyfully. Robert lifted her off the ground, swung her around, and held her close, burying his nose into her hair.

With tears on his cheeks he exclaimed, "You've gone and grown right up, Ruthie!" and he covered her face with kisses and set her down. Finally, his eyes went to Helen, whose hands were at her mouth to hold back audible sobs.

"My love and my life, my beloved wife," he grinned with that same grin that always melted Helen's heart. Then he held out his arms for her, "Come here and make me whole again!" This was his greeting for Helen for as long as the children could remember whether he was gone for a day or a year.

Robert was straight and strong with a gentle yet imposing face. You knew he was a fair man just by looking at him. Claire couldn't imagine anybody being so bold as to cross him, yet there he stood with his family around, his wife in his arms; crying, unashamed of his affection and devotion towards his family. Claire's stomach stopped flopping and she already felt at ease with this man.

When at last the family caught their breath and the initial rush of emotion had settled, Robert turned towards Claire and said, "Please excuse me, young lady, I did not mean to ignore you." He wiped his eyes and asked, "Helen? Who is our guest?"

"My love, I would like to introduce you to Claire, a gift from the sea." Helen winked toward Robert, "Claire, this is Mr. Harrington."

Robert laughed, "That sounds like a story!" He then took Claire by both hands; bent a bit at the knees so as to look her straight in the eyes and told her "You must call me Robert, please." With a blush, Claire nodded.

"Do you need to stay in town a bit to take care of anything before you can come home?" Helen inquired.

"No, I'll take care of it tomorrow. O'Connell and Franklin volunteered to stay aboard for the night." Robert answered.

"Wonderful," Helen beamed, "Let's get ourselves home."

"Can I help you, sir?" asked Franklin as Mr. Orson approached the captain's office aboard the 'Helena'.

"Uh, yes, I'm Mr. Orson. I own the financial institution here in town; therefore, I'm part owner of this ship. I thought I knew all of Captain Harrington's crew. Who are you, and why don't I know you?" Mr. Orson huffed.

"The name's Franklin, sir. I'm a cousin of O'Connell, from farther up north. I joined the crew just this trip, and I was late signing, but since my cousin recommended me the Captain let me on, sir. It has been an amazing opportunity, sir, Captain Harrington is," Franklin was explaining but Mr. Orson interrupted.

"Yes, yes, that's fine young man. As the good Captain did not see that the manifests were brought to me before he went home, and we will need to unload and shift and all types of work will need to be done starting very early tomorrow, I'd like to get a look at them before I retire for the evening, so I will have an idea where to start tomorrow." He told young Franklin, sounding very put out.

Mr. Orson stood at the door to the captain's cabin looking dismissively at young Franklin. Poor Franklin became very uncomfortable, looked down at his feet, and cleared his throat.

"Um, yes sir," he mumbled as he took two steps awkwardly back, "I'll be, um, just over…" looking over his shoulder and pointing aimlessly, "over there, sir."

"Ye-ess." Mr. Orson replied in his very curt manner.

Once inside the office, it didn't take Mr. Orson long to reach his goal. He knew exactly which drawer Captain Harrington kept the ledgers in. Each port stop had a separate ledger containing the history and accounts of that particular stop. Each listed all purchases, sales, and other notes, such as names and customs pertaining to that area. Mr. Orson was mostly interested in the numbers. Not the people behind them.

He scanned through them quickly and took a ledger from one of the ports that had the intermediary amount of business, feeling this would be less obvious. He took both copies so that the captain would not have a backup. Double-checking to see if he was being watched at the door, he slipped them into an inside pocket of his suit jacket and left feeling well pleased with his cleverness.

"Will that be all, Mr. Orson?" Franklin asked as Mr. Orson walked out past him.

"Yes, quite. Good evening Frankman." Mr. Orson sneered back without even looking at him.

"Franklin sir." Franklin quietly corrected the back of Mr. Orson's uncaring head.

12

ROBERT AND KYLE and some of the local crew returned to the ship the following day to start the process of unloading the cargo from the ship to storage; organizing and cataloging. Besides the physical need to get it off the ship and into storage, it was mostly inventory. But as Captain Harrington was very organized in his paperwork, organizing it was fairly easy work; made even more so since Kyle had been loading and unloading at the docks more this season. His father taught him well.

Captain Harrington went to his cabin to retrieve his ledgers. Two were missing. Looking through the drawers and ledgers again, noticing that two of the same ledgers were missing. He dug around under his desk, through the other drawers, cabinets, tables, and shelves. He tore apart his bed, looking under, around, and behind it. He looked everywhere he could possibly think of. Did he leave it at a port he wondered as he sat at the end of his bed, scanning the room for what he may have missed. No, no, he was sure he hadn't. He got up and went outside and saw O'Connell.

"O'Connell," he called.

"Yes, Captain?"

"Was there anyone in my cabin last night?"

"Well, yes sir. Mr. Orson dropped in. I was in the galley setting up supper for my cousin, Franklin, and myself. Franklin said Mr. Orson wanted to get an early look at the books sir, seeing as you hadn't stopped by. Is there a problem, sir? Would you like me to get Franklin?"

"No, no, O'Connell. It's alright. That's all, then? You're sure?" Robert asked somewhat distractedly.

"Yes sir, I brought our supper up here to Franklin and we ate right here. Slept right here too, sir. It was a beautiful night. Quiet the rest of the evening sir." O'Connell assured his captain.

"Very good, thank you, O'Connell. Let's get back to work then shall we?" Robert grabbed O'Connell good-naturedly by the shoulder and smiled, putting the man at ease.

Captain Harrington gave the men instruction to unload only from the existing ledgers; they weren't going to unload them all just yet; that there was an issue with some of the cargo that needed his attention before it could be unloaded. He clarified what was to go and what was to stay without actually telling them yet that some of the ledgers were missing. He had his suspicions about what had happened to them but didn't think it wise for many reasons to reveal them. He needn't wait long before his suspicions were confirmed.

Mr. Orson met Robert on the street between docks about mid-day. He wasn't one for rising early or getting his hands dirty with the labor end of trade.

"Robert!" he greeted enthusiastically, "Welcome home man. That is quite a shipment you brought in this time. This must be one of your biggest yet, eh? Do you have a set of records for me so I can get started on that paperwork?"

"Yes Dale I do, but there seems to be a problem," Robert answered, keeping his tone informal and friendly. He watched Mr. Orson's reaction to this news carefully. Robert was good at reading people, and Mr. Orson, or Dale as Robert called him, was not as clever as he thought he was. Because of his position, he just intimidated most people, but Robert knew Mr. Orson too well and was not intimidated by the spurious man.

Mr. Orson's eyes opened a little too wide. His eyebrows arched a little too high, and his mouth dropped a little too low.

"Re-ally?" he inquired with all the sincerity he could muster, "What might that be?"

With Robert's suspicions confirmed, he answered, "It seems that a single set of ledgers are missing."

"How unfortunate, Robert. You are usually so organized. I hope you find them soon. I'll check in with you tomorrow." Mr. Orson sympathized.

"If I find them sooner Dale, I'll stop them by the bank." Robert tested.

"Yes, yes, of course, that too," was Mr. Orson's reply as he was walking away waving Robert off.

Robert decided not to mention anything to the family when he and Kyle returned home for dinner. He wanted to see how this played out for the next couple of days. He was sure that Mr. Orson would present his motives soon and he wanted to make sure they were what he thought they were.

The Harrington family had a wonderful evening at home. After dinner, the men went out and tended to the evening chores while the women finished in the house. Claire made one of her berry pies, this time adding some dried apples cut up very small to the berries to enjoy after supper. During supper, the family drilled Robert about his trip. He always had great stories about the interesting people he'd met and the things that he brought back. His first night back, they had a large spiky fruit that when you cut it open revealed a bright yellow juicy flesh that was tart and sweet all at once. Ruth said it burned her tongue. Robert had called it a pineapple, which he thought was the funniest thing. It looked nothing like an apple. It looked like nothing they had seen at all!

Summer had arrived and the evening was warm, but not too warm yet. There was a breeze coming over the hill carrying the slight scent of the ocean. The sky was still light, although the hour was getting late and you could still see and hear the occasional shrill call of a seagull.

They all sat outside on the front porch enjoying the pie and the sounds of the evening. Helen and Robert sitting close on the porch swing. Helen teased Robert that she was about to be jealous of the fuss he was making over the pie, but she was only teasing. She was proud of Claire.

"I can't wait to see what she can do with the apples this fall," Kyle added to Claire's delight. "Dad, you should taste what she can do with a simple soup; and her casserole bread!"

"Sounds like you just made a request for tomorrow's dinner." Helen teased.

"Yes. Did you bring home olives this time, Dad? Claire, wait until you taste an olive; or maybe you have?"

"No, I don't think so." Claire laughed.

"Mmmm, the big black kind." Kyle closed his eyes with a hum at the thought of them.

Having their father home had animated the family. Claire had not realized how much they had missed him before because they didn't complain. His effect on the family was intoxicating. They all felt like a whole again. Claire found that she was falling in love with this family more than ever. Sitting there watching Kyle work on his latest jewelry box, Ruth struggling with her needlepoint, Helen and Robert just sitting close, Helen's head on Robert's shoulder looking out over their home from the porch swing; she felt a ripple of contentment creep through her muscles. She hadn't realized how tense she always was until that moment. She realized she was feeling a little more comfortable in her skin. Maybe just a little more.

The next morning after eating eggs and the rest of the pie for breakfast, Kyle and Robert walked back down to the docks to finish working. By mid-morning, as Robert thought would happen, Mr. Orson came walking up to Robert on the street between the docks again. This time his approach was more businesslike.

"So, Robert," he started soberly, "any news on your missing ledgers?"

"No Dale. No sign of them." Robert countered.

"Most unfortunate, most unfortunate." Mr. Orson clicked with his head down to show sorrow. Putting his arm around Robert's shoulder was uncomfortable because Robert was much taller than Mr. Orson; he led Robert away, down the street so they could have some privacy. Robert was almost amused by this development.

Dropping his arm and standing beside Robert, Mr. Orson started, "Robert, as your friend, I feel like I should warn you about the consequences if you cannot produce these ledgers. The trade committee meeting is next month, as you know, and we are hosting it right here in our little town. Of course, you know all this, seeing as you are the president of the committee.

I would have to report your discrepancies to the committee for review. If word got out that we made an exception for you and it could you know, wasn't it you who pushed for the open book policy? Yes, well no matter. If word got out that I had made an exception, then you know that there are those who would take advantage and try a little cheating of their own. Not that I believe that you are doing that at all, Robert. Please do not misunderstand me, I trust you completely, but there are others. If you were to be put in front of the review board, you could very well be placed on probation and lose your license to sail or trade or maybe both. Who knows?"

Mr. Orson paused, waiting to see if Robert would respond. He didn't. He just looked Mr. Orson in the eyes without contention, just a slight hint of interest. Rattled as Robert intended, Mr. Orson continued a little less certain of himself than before.

"As your friend Robert, naturally I am concerned for the welfare of you and your family. But I am a businessman."

Here it comes, thought Robert as Mr. Orson pressed on.

"You could lose your ship; you still owe me on it. If you lose your ship, you will lose your livelihood, and how would you support your family? I wouldn't want to lose my best sea merchant either. I would hate to see you lose your ship; honestly, it would cost me a lot of money. You know that I have always been covetous of your property Robert. My offer is this, I would buy your land, giving you enough money to purchase something smaller straight across, and I would dissolve what you owe on your ship. You would be out of debt, and the ship would still be yours to sail if you don't lose that privilege after the review. You think about it Robert, the committee won't be here for a month."

"Thank you, Dale. It seems you've put quite a deal of thought into my interest." Robert flattered, "I will give it the thought it deserves and get back to you. I'm not giving up on finding the ledgers quite yet."

"Of course, of course." Mr. Orson placated. "Better to cover our bases. I'll talk to you soon Robert, send my greetings to your family."

That night Robert informed his family about the ledgers and the conversation with Mr. Orson. The family was upset, reasonably so, and all reacted in their personal ways as Robert had expected. And this amused Robert to a degree. Ruth had many colorful words to say about dear Mr. Orson and when she calmed down had to be reminded about respect and tolerance. Kyle curled his hands into fists, nostrils flared. His breathing became heavier but he remained quiet. Claire had never seen him angry, and it looked strange on him. Helen just nodded quietly and listened. Claire was scared for the family and wasn't sure what to do. When all was quiet Robert added, "Have faith family, I don't have an answer right now, but we will be given one, I'm sure of it. We won't be left alone. For now, we'll keep our eyes and ears open."

Claire and the young Harringtons went to bed, not feeling much like socializing, while Robert and Helen went for a walk around the property.

"Helen, I've seen that we will not lose our property. I'm not sure how it will come about, that part is unclear, but we will not lose our property." Robert assured her, putting his arm around her shoulder and pulling her close.

"Alright love, then I'll give it no more worry." Resting her head against his chest and wrapping both arms around his middle, Helen collaborated, "eyes and ears open."

13

A T BREAKFAST, THE FAMILY was pretty quiet. Helen and Robert tried to keep the mood optimistic.

"The street market starts next weekend," Helen said.

"Do you have enough things put together for it?" Robert inquired.

"Oh sure, I have about ten nightgowns done, some pillows, and one large quilt. Ruth's berries are so full this year! Kyle, you have about four of your jewelry boxes done and just as many brush sets? A couple of other little trinket boxes too, right? Claire is planning to bake up some pies the day before. We should give out samples. Nobody would be able to resist." Helen continued.

"That'll be a good start," Robert replied before pausing a minute. He then grinned, and turning to Kyle said, "Kyle, why don't you take Claire fishing today?"

Kyle and Claire, Ruth and Helen too, for that matter, looked at Robert in surprise who just kept picking at his biscuit innocently without looking up.

"What about work today, dad?" Kyle protested.

"We're almost done, son. Have you ever been fishing, Claire?" Claire shook her head no in response to Robert's question. "Alright then." And with that, Robert smiled at his family, put his dish in the sink, kissed his wife, and went into town.

Kyle and Claire started for town, both nervous. They had never really spent time alone together. Although they were at ease and talked readily at home, surrounded by family, this felt different. Claire was also nervous about going out on the water in this small boat. She had only dipped her toes off the docks with Helen since Kyle had pulled her from the water. She felt unease near the open water. Either connected with her dreams and visions or the unknown just lurking associated with her near-drowning and why she was even there in the first palace. She felt torn between letting go of the unknown and living in the present and an unexplainable embarrassment of what was before.

As they got to the dock, Claire was yanked from her anxious train of thought as they approached Kyle's little boat. Claire had not realized that the name she plucked off the side of the boat 'Claire' in desperation, was Kyle's boat! Releasing an audible gasp, Claire flushed red as she looked at Kyle with a feeling of guilt. Kyle noticed what she had seen and had a nervous, guilty look on his face too. They both cast their eyes down, looking at their shoes.

This is your boat?" Claire asks, breaking the silence.

"Um, yes," he answered timidly.

Kyle helped Claire in then got in himself and pushed them off the dock. Kyle rowed, nervously avoiding eye contact with Claire, guiding his boat within the inlet almost to the mouth until he found his favorite fishing spot.

Both were quiet as Kyle set up his fishing gear, chancing glances at Claire who was staring thoughtfully out to sea, privately hoping she hadn't offended Kyle with her reaction upon seeing that "Claire" was actually *his* boat. How could she explain?

Making a couple of casts into the water, Kyle waited, reeling in the line, and casting again. The water was smooth, the sun was out, and it was another gorgeous day. The seagulls were circling high, looking for cast-off bait they could utilize, providing a welcome distraction to Claire's tumbling thoughts. Claire liked these squawking birds; the way they would tilt their heads quizzically and argue with each other. Claire was feeling less nervous about being on the water than she had been. With the gentle rock of the water, the sound of it slapping the side of the boat rhythmically, she began to relax. She closed her eyes and soaked it all in, taking advantage of the moment without chores to consider or, well, everything.

Kyle watched her for a while, wondering what was going on in her mind before breaking the silence and asking, "Claire, what are you thinking about?" Feeling embarrassed now that she was looking at him thoughtfully, he added, "I mean, you don't need to tell me. You just, you just looked deep in thought. It's not my business. Never mind, I'm sorry." And he checked his line unnecessarily.

Head tilted, Claire contemplated Kyle's request a moment before deciding to respond, "You will surely think I'm crazy, too much seawater before you pulled me to shore." She excused.

"I'd like to hear… Will you trust me?" Kyle returned.

Tentatively she started to tell him about her dreams of the ocean, little red fish in tall white wigs. At the mention of the fish, Kyle tightened slightly, just enough for Claire to notice. He hadn't even meant to. Claire blushed and stared again at the bottom of the boat.

"I know, it sounds so crazy." She apologized, misinterpreting his reaction.

"No, I'm sorry. Please continue." He appealed and put his hand on her knee reassuringly, not meaning to do that either.

Claire returned to her narrative with the face of a curly, dark-haired girl, loving parents, and the overly powdered man. How the girl is spoiled and thoughtless, causing them their demise. It all seems real but is all so different from what she knows here and seems like a dream. It was such a relief to say it all out loud to Kyle and not feel judged. Kyle just listened. She told him how she had felt she didn't actually belong here. Like an imposter.

Kyle sat there and looked at Claire for a moment, lost in thought, until Claire became self-conscious and looked out at the water.

"You know Claire, I'm not sure what to make of your dreams. I guess only you can decide what they mean. I could read something different into them just because of my experiences. But I could share some stories that I know, they may be of some help or just entertaining." He grinned when Claire looked back at him with a smile, pleased that he had simply accepted her stories.

Kyle then told Claire about the stories of long ago and across the sea how men of means and importance would wear these silly wigs and ornate clothing. He told of the old sailor's stories and songs of Calypso the sea goddess of folklore and fairy tales, and the old sea men's superstitions. Of how Calypso would listen at the side of the ships and toy with the people's lives for she had existed as long as the sea itself. She could crush even the largest of ships in one hand on a whim, sending its passengers off onto another life journey or keeping them at the bottom of the sea.

"But I, the dreams, the visions, it all seems so real," Claire confided.

Kyle was quiet and thoughtful for a time, reeling the line back in, re-baiting and casting out again, then timidly at first, becoming more confident as he looked up into her eyes, finally setting his fishing pole aside, and told her of his own dream.

"I'm in the ocean swimming out to sea searching for something, but I'm not sure what, just knowing that I had to get to it and quickly, with my very life, I needed to find this, I was about to give up, I was growing tired, when three little red fish wearing what looked like tall white wigs floated by and one said to me a single word 'Claire'. At this point, I always woke up. I had never known a Claire, nor had my mother heard of a Claire in any nearby village, but it haunted me. Four years ago, on my 15th birthday, my father presented me with this very boat. I couldn't imagine anything in the world that would make me any happier or that I would want any more, so I named her Claire." He stopped himself for a second, having just embarrassed himself, but continued, saying, "I had just been out fishing that day I found you, I had *just* rowed past that *very* spot I had pulled you from and I swear you weren't there! How could I have missed you? I'm sure there is no way I could have! But as I was tying my boat to the dock I caught a movement out of the corner of my eye and heard that silly little fish in my head." At this, he grinned, "he said simply 'Claire' so I dove in, and here you are. Well, imagine how my heart stopped when you told me your name was Claire."

At this, Claire put her face in her hands and began to cry, releasing the tears she had felt at the edge of her tear ducts from that first day. "But I'm not even Claire," she confessed, "I saw it on your boat!"

Kyle took her hand and wiped the tears from her cheeks and palms, saying, "But you are Claire, the Claire foretold in my dreams, I do not doubt that now."

His fishing pole gave a tug, interrupting the tender moment.

"You've got a bite!" Claire exclaimed.

Kyle's easy smile returned to his face as he grabbed the pole to reel in their prize. It was a little too easy to bring in. "I think I've just snagged something" Kyle announced disappointedly, and indeed he had.

As he brought his catch to the boat, they saw a waterlogged but exquisite woman's shoe. A lovely light blue velvet pair of shoes with ethereal hand-embroidered flowers in multiple shades of blues and lavender. Crystal beadwork and small gems were elegantly worked into the design. The type that would be worn by a girl who was now considered to be a young woman.

"I know that shoe," Claire said with a far-off look, slowly reaching for the shoe. "I know what to do." She said more to herself.

Kyle handed her the shoe looking from the shoe to Claire curiously. Claire turned it over in her hands, studying it for a moment thoughtfully.

"Please don't tell anybody about the shoe Kyle, not even your parents. Please, trust me, I know what I need to do," was all Claire offered in explanation.

"Alright," Kyle agreed.

14

COME SATURDAY THE FAMILY was ready for opening day at the street market. They loaded their goods in the back of the wagon, bringing a couple of chairs, a small table, and as many small plates and forks, as they could find for serving samples of Claire's pies. They decided to throw in a small washbasin to clean the dishes. Helen was sure they could get water from the bakery. Also in the back of the wagon was a trunk holding the nightgowns, a crate full of berries, and a crate loaded with Kyle's boxes and brush sets. Poor Sunrise, she was such a good sport. They tried to make sure the wagon wasn't too heavy, but to be sure, the family chose to walk with Sunrise so as not to overburden her.

As luck would have it, or design, the Harrington family was nearly one of the first vendors to set up, so they picked their favorite spot just at the beginning of the street where everybody must enter and leave. A nice grassy area was arranged behind the stables for the vendor's horses if they behaved (the horses, not the vendors, although that pertained to the vendors too). Kyle took Sunrise to the designated area and then went to the docks to check in with his dad, who had gone to the 'Helena' while the women then finished arranging their goods. On the small table, they placed a lovely embroidered tablecloth to serve the pie samples. Kyle's boxes and brush sets were displayed in the back of the wagon, along with Ruth's berries. The trunk holding the nightgowns was sitting on the ground, and Helen's quilts were laid over the sides of the wagon. The Harringtons were ready for business.

Mary from the bakery came out to say hello to Helen and the girls. Mary often bought some of Ruth's berries for making pastries and pies in her bakery. Trying a sample of Claire's pie, Mary was impressed, teasing Claire that she would need to hire her to make pies for the bakery to eliminate the competition. She then bought a nightgown for her daughter stating, "She is so spoiled by your nightgowns Helen, nothing else will do." After buying quite a few berries from Ruth, she wished them luck, gave hugs, and returned to work.

Up and down the street, below the boardwalks, vendors were setting up their wares. There were more quilts and canned goods, flowers and jewelry, homemade soaps and oils, horse tackle, and fishing tackle. There was always such a variety of goods, the selections changing through the season.

Ruth stayed at the wagon while Helen took Claire up and down the street to meet some of the other vendors. It was an opportunity to see friends and acquaintances that they hadn't seen since the holiday socials or even last season. When they passed the bank, they took the opportunity to get some change for the day's sales.

Mr. Spencer, Mr. Orson's employee at the bank, was working behind the counter. Mr. Spencer was, in contrast to Mr. Orson, a taller, thin man with friendly eyes and a meek appearance. He almost reminded Claire of a mouse in his mannerism, but she liked him. Helen introduced him to Claire and he greeted her in a squeaky voice bidding them luck at the market as they were leaving. Mr. Orson caught sight of them as he was coming down the stairs from his large apartment above the bank. Helen and Claire also saw him and walked faster towards the door pretending not to see him, managing to escape without having to talk to him.

Things were getting busy at the market; Ruth had sold one of Kyle's brush sets while Helen and Claire were gone. The street market was always a very social time, and the people were out visiting and catching up with friends. The vendors traded goods amongst themselves and bought from each other, making the atmosphere light and pleasant. It was nearing dinner time, and the sun was high overhead.

Mr. Orson strolled down the street absently looking at the vendor's wares ending up, not surprisingly, at the Harrington's wagon.

"Good afternoon, ladies. Oh, what have we here?" he inquired, looking keenly at the pies.

"Berry pies, Mr. Orson. Claire makes them. Would you like a sample?" Helen answered.

"I can't think of anything I'd like better." He replied with a small unappealing chortle looking right at Claire. A little bile rose into her throat.

Of course, he enjoyed his sample of pie, complete with repulsive lip-smacking noises and much licking of the lips. He then bought a pie and made himself comfortable on one of the women's chairs.

"You know Claire," he started most importantly, "I have an eye for what is of great value. I pride myself on my ability to pick out the gems from the stones. These pies are like you in a way. They have a hidden quality that is intriguing." His eyes were boring into her, looking her over in a most uncomfortable way as he continued, "Like a hidden treasure. I do like to acquire treasure…" he faded off.

"Yes, well, will there be anything else for you today Mr. Orson?" Helen interrupted as she put herself between his leering and Claire.

"Could I interest you in some lunch Claire?" he asked.

"Yes, I suppose you call it dinner; seeing as you are, well, farmers. Farmers and peasants, it's an old tradition I suppose, but those who are a bit more cultured, no offense meant, call it lunch," was Mr. Orson's extremely ill-worded and pompous response.

"Peasants, who says peasants? What the…" was the start of Ruth's sardonic reply, cut short as Robert and Kyle joined the family, to Helen's relief. Robert crossed in front of Mr. Orson and gave Helen a big kiss on the top of her head, and announced, "We thought we could head over to the bakery and see what they are cooking up for *dinner*! You gals hungry?" The tension the women were feeling was broken as Robert used the word dinner. Laughing, they all agreed that sounded like a wonderful idea. Helen gave Robert an extra kiss and hug for his perfect timing.

Robert beamed, "Okay then, I'll buy you dinner more often!"

"Do you think that is wise Robert, considering your… situation?" Mr. Orson jibed.

Robert just looked at Mr. Orson without a hint of anger and continued, "Let's order and bring it back here for a picnic. Kyle, would you mind holding down the station while we go get some food? You will excuse us, Dale, won't you?"

Mr. Orson knew he was being dismissed He thanked them for the pie and started back with a huff. He stopped, looking apathetically at more vendors as he returned up the street, hoping it wouldn't be too obvious that he had only come out today to try and impress Claire.

Dinner was a delicious meal of hard rolls, loose meat served with early crop greens, gingered ice tea, and easy conversation.

"Would it be alright if Ruth and I walked down the beach a way and explored a bit?" Claire asked, adding, "I've never been down that direction before."

Ruth was very excited to be the one invited, and she took Claire's hand and pulled her away before even receiving permission, not they wouldn't have received it. Claire laughed; she loved this enthusiastic little girl.

Past the church, the girls stopped to take off their shoes, strolling commodiously, looking around for whole sand dollars and interesting pieces of driftwood. They spotted the occasional little crab scurrying sideways in a hurry so as not to attract the attention of the hunting gulls above. The girls chased the small waves in and out, only trying meagerly to keep from getting their feet wet. When the girls were giggled out and had found a nice log to sit on, Claire asked, "Ruth, would you like to help me with something?"

"Sure! What?"

"How would you like to help me get Mr. Orson to stop bothering your family?"

"Our family," Ruth interrupted.

The correction stopped Claire short for a moment. Regaining her thoughts, she continued, "Bothering *the* family, about the land and hopefully solve the mystery about the missing ledgers?"

"YES!"

"Alright, I have a plan, but I must ask you not to say a word to anybody. Anybody Ruth, can you do that? If it is going to work, it has to be just between you and me." Claire informed Ruth most emphatically. It was hard for Claire to act in such a contrived manner and pull Ruth into it too, but she knew that the others would not allow it, trying to protect her. But this could work. She just knew it. She was scared to death, but she knew this could work.

"I promise, Claire. I absolutely promise!" was Ruth's emphatic reply.

That next week was a nervous week for Ruth and Claire, waiting to put their plan into action, but they kept busy, and happily, the family kept busy as always also. Robert needed to go to town a couple of times to do some maintenance on the ship. He took Kyle along for extra help and a chance to teach him as well. Helen made berry preserves and taught Claire, with Ruth's help. Claire was pleased with how comfortable she was feeling with the work of keeping a home. The tomatoes were coming on in the garden turning a stunning red. They sliced them up one evening for supper. They served them with black olives marinated in oil with peppers and spices that Robert had brought back for the family. Kyle was beside himself, piling the rich mixture atop slices of fresh baked and toasted bread, clearing his plate of the oil and herbs, and helping himself to even more bread.

One day, Robert filleted and smoked two big fish they had caught, in his homemade smoker, using sugar-browned with molasses they picked up at the market. Helen and Claire took advantage of the browned sugar and had made cinnamon rolls the day before. The corn was growing tall, although the ears were still relatively small for this time of the growing season. That was just fine though, smaller ears were usually sweeter. They would have plenty to take to market that coming weekend.

Robert and Kyle traveled north one day to Mr. Marshall's to check if he would need any extra help bringing in his hay this year. He was glad for their offer; his oldest boy had gone to the big city looking for work so he could attend university in the fall. He was going to be a doctor, Mr. Marshall added with great pride, "Can you believe it? One of my boys going to a university and learning to be a doctor. Says he'll come back here to set up his practice so we can have one closer."

Ready or not, the second weekend of the market arrived, and the Harrington family set out and set up as usual. It was another beautiful day, but that wasn't unusual for this time of year. Claire felt sick and nervous. This was the day. Claire was sure Helen would notice her shaking hands despite the smile she was trying to wear. Robert and Kyle had to go to the storehouses to fill an order for the general store.

Just as it was nearing dinner time again, Claire took a deep breath, braced herself, and asked Helen if she would mind if she took another pie to Mr. Orson. She could take Ruth as an escort. Helen thought this request was a little queer and studied the girls a moment, her head slightly tilted for what was a very uncomfortable amount of time, making Claire and Ruth fidgety. Neither of the girls wanted to deceive Helen, and they were praying that she wouldn't ask questions, and she didn't. She just answered slowly and thoughtfully, "Okay."

The girls grabbed a pie walking away quickly without looking back, both feeling guilty but determined in what they had to do. When they were sure they were out of earshot, Claire checked with Ruth, "Are you ready? I won't be mad if you want to go back Ruthie, I really won't. I will understand."

"No way Claire, I'm not going to back out," was Ruth's brave reply.

Claire was relieved and distressed at the same time. It wouldn't work without Ruth's help. This was so beyond anything Claire ever dreamed she was capable of even considering. Yet, here she was and taking Ruth with her. She just kept telling herself that it was for the Harrington family. She had to do this for the Harrington family. She *could* do this if only for the Harrington family.

Mr. Spencer was behind the counter as the girls entered the bank.

"Hello ladies, you need more change already?" he asked.

"No sir, thank you," Claire answered, "Is Mr. Orson in?"

"Yes, he's in his office. Is he expecting you?" Mr. Spencer asked officially.

"No, he's not expecting us, but could you let him know that Claire is here with an, um, a gift," Claire answered, trying not to sound as uneasy as she was feeling.

Mr. Spencer looked at the girls with an expression very similar to the one Helen had just given them before going to Mr. Orson's office door knocking lightly, almost apprehensively. From behind the door came Mr. Orson's gruff reply, "Come in!"

Mr. Spencer stepped tentatively into Mr. Orson's office, shutting the door slightly behind him. You could hear their muffled exchange and Claire turned to Ruth saying, "Okay, Ruth this is it." Claire proclaimed as she swallowed back the urge to vomit. Her heart was in her ears, and she could feel the strength in her legs leaving her. "We can still back out. We can just give him the pie and go."

Ruth teased, "Are you chicken, Claire? I'm not chicken. Ready?"

Ruth was amazing. She had a grin on her face like she was quite enjoying this. *'Oh Ruth,'* Claire thought. *What have I gotten you into? You amaze me."*

"Ready." Claire grinned back at her, borrowing some of Ruth's nerve.

"He'll be right with you." Mr. Spencer said as he returned to his position behind the counter. Claire thought she saw him roll his eyes as he turned towards the counter, and she had to grin.

Shortly after, Mr. Orson came strutting out of his office. He seemed even more puffed up than usual as he exclaimed,

"Well, well, what a delightful surprise." Then, "Oh," as he noticed Ruth, obviously annoyed by the discovery of her presence.

"I was just wondering, Mr. Orson, if that invitation to lunch was still available." Claire stated with as much feminine charm as she could muster, "I brought you another pie." She wasn't sure she even knew how to flirt and felt very silly.

Mr. Orson's powder-pale face looked very pleased yet annoyed and smug as he continued to look down at Ruth as if she were a stain on his floor. Ruth simply returned his gaze, managing to look both innocent and eager for the opportunity to dine with the esteemed Mr. Orson.

"Of course Mr. Orson, it would only be proper if Ruth came as my escort," Claire offered.

Mr. Orson's sour response was, "Of course. Spencer! I'll be taking lunch. Do not disturb me." He glowered. Then as if by hitting a switch, Mr. Orson's expression and demeanor changed from annoyed and intimidating to amiable and cheerful as he led the girls up the stairs.

For a moment anyway, until they reached the top of the stairs and stepped through the door leading to his large apartment, and he bellowed,

"OLIVIA! OLIVIA!" and as she appeared from what may have been the kitchen door, "Tea in the library for three to start, then bring us lunch followed by some of this lovely pie." At the last part about the pie, he glanced towards Claire, which may have been meant as a flirtatious raise of the eyebrows causing Olivia to look quickly from Mr. Orson and to the girls, wide-eyed with alarm, before schooling her reaction and responding, "Yes, Mr. Orson."

The three walked down the familiar hall towards the library, Mr. Orson repeating his well-rehearsed opportunity to impress about the artwork and collections that lined the walls, of their great worth and the great lengths at which he had to go to acquire them.

The girls nodded dutifully, acting appropriately impressed all the way into the library. Mr. Orson led the girls into the library, standing by his roll-top secretary's desk near the door, allowing the girls to be, again impressed, with this great room. It was an admittedly remarkable room, long and ending with a bay window with a glass door to its left. The door led to the balcony Claire had noticed above the bank that first day she came to town with Helen and Ruth to buy dresses. The view was striking, surveying the water over the top of the shops across the street and beyond the storage buildings. You could see the ships that were docked and undoubtedly others as they came in and out. The walls of the library were lined with shelves, not to hold books so much as to hold collections. There were many books of course, but as Mr. Orson soon explained, they were of great value not for the stories they held (at least not to him) but for their rarity.

"Do you see that rather large, old book there," he pointed, "that particular tome is all handwritten, way before the time of printing presses. Handwritten and painted, in gold leaf, by some monk somewhere, I have it documented, long since dead. Very rare, very valuable."

"What is it about?" Ruth asked innocently.

"How should I know? That's not the point." Mr. Orson snapped at her 'obvious' ignorance.

He continued to prattle on a bit about a couple more paintings when Claire asked, wanting to get this over with but trying to be careful; she did not want it to seem like she had an agenda, "How do you keep track of all of it? I mean, how do you know what it's all worth?"

Mr. Orson strolled over to his roll-top desk, stroked it with his fingertips along the roll-top's ridges, and laughing at his own joke answered, "I have every piece cataloged and documented. I like to keep my most important papers close by. Banks get broken into."

Claire looked to Ruth, who understood and nodded ever so slightly. Claire then walked over to the velvet shoe she had seen before, which had caused her that strange vertigo and hint of remembrance. It was kept in a locked glass case on a shelf centered on the left wall. A lamp hung above it that could be lit when needed for better viewing. Claire got that strange feeling of déjà vu again, only it was just a mere suggestion this time, barely a ghost of a thought. This buoyed her resolve somehow. This plan will work, she told herself, taking a deep breath.

"This is so beautiful. I've been thinking about it since I was here with Helen." Claire flattered.

"Yes. That is my most valuable piece." He explained, "It is dated back over one hundred years. I had it authenticated by two leading historians and a well-respected art authority and restorer. It is absolutely priceless. What makes it so priceless is the fact that it is so old for one thing, but moreover, it was found in the sea. There are all kinds of traces of minerals and things that would indicate it, yet it is in almost perfect condition. The threads are intact and the beading hasn't been worn down, the leather is almost as strong as if it were made only a few years ago. Completely unexplainable. Lucky for me, the fishermen that brought it to me had no idea what they had, and I practically stole it from them."

At this moment in his explanation, Olivia entered with the tea for three. It was hard to say what Olivia's age was. She looked like she may be younger than she appeared if only she didn't have that discontented look on her face. She was pleasant-looking and somewhat plump. She looked as if she could be quite cheery if she had a mind to be, but she did work for Mr. Orson, so that may explain it.

"It's such a beautiful day, and your view from the balcony seems quite striking. Would you mind if we took our tea outside?" suggested Claire.

Olivia obediently started towards the glass door with the tea, following Mr. Orson and Claire. Ruth cleared her throat hesitantly and quietly announced that she was afraid of heights and would prefer to stay inside.

"Of course Ruthie, you could sit here, and then you can still see us," Claire said, indicating the two wingback chairs on either side of the small table nestled in the nook of the bay window. Ruth chose the seat that was turned away from the balcony. Not because she was afraid to look outside, because she really wasn't afraid of heights at all, she was just very clever, but so *they* could not see *her* as well from the balcony. Olivia sat the tea tray outside on the small table between two chairs looking over the town then took a cup of tea and saucer into Ruth, shutting the glass door before leaving the library.

Claire chose the chair farthest from the windows hoping to draw Mr. Orson's attention away from the library. She sat and sipped her tea quietly, Mr. Orson in the chair opposite her. He would glance over the top of his teacup at her, smiling wolfishly as he slurped his tea with his pinky in the air. His smile was not warm and seemed unnatural on his face, but Claire grinned back, taking comfort in the knowledge that they could be seen from the street. She wasn't sure that Mr. Orson's honor could be counted on otherwise.

"You have a lovely place Mr. Orson, and so many lovely things. I'm surprised you don't have anyone to share it with." She grimaced at her own words and the image they brought, quickly bringing a napkin to her mouth to hide her reaction, hoping he hadn't noticed. He hadn't.

"Yes, well, I like to have the best, as I've said. And I haven't found anything I would find intriguing enough to consider." He oozed, adding, "Until recently."

Claire almost choked on her tea. Coughing a little, she took the opportunity to look over and see if she could see Ruth. Ruth was no longer in the chair. *'Oh my goodness,'* she thought. *'Be careful, Ruth.'*

"Really, she would be a lucky woman," Claire responded, then getting up to walk a little further down the balcony, anxious to get away from the bay windows and glass door. She attempted to change the subject. Mr. Orson was pleased with what he thought was Claire's attempt to get away from the eyes of her escort.

Ruth was almost to the secretary's desk when she caught their movement out of the corner of her eye, and she froze mid-step. As they disappeared beyond the glass door, she let out her breath, not realizing she was holding it, and continued towards the desk.

Out on the balcony, Claire was asking, "Mr. Orson, tell me, how does a man like you become so successful?"

Mr. Orson was more than happy to go on about his brilliance, allowing Ruth the opportunity to put her part of the plan into action. Ruth rolled up the desktop and began leafing through all of the papers. Luckily for Ruth and Claire, Mr. Orson was very organized, and everything was very clearly marked. Ruth was digging into the fourth divider, when the door from the hall opened, revealing Olivia with the sandwiches. Ruth froze once again, watching for Olivia's reaction, trying unsuccessfully to come up with a quick reason to be ruffling through Mr. Orson's desk. She chastised herself for not waiting until after the sandwiches were served. She had forgotten about the darn sandwiches in her nerves. Olivia stopped, looked at Ruth for a moment, caught red-handed, before continuing towards the glass door leading out to the balcony. Ruth was too scared to move. Claire jumped a little when Olivia walked out onto the balcony and silently served the sandwiches, watching Olivia for any sign of trouble. Had Ruth heard her coming? Had she been caught? What would they do? How could they get out of this?

To Ruth, it seemed an hour before Olivia returned, though it had only been a few moments. Claire just waited, her heart about to explode from her chest, sure the flush she felt run up her neck and cheeks would give her away, trying to act normal, hoping Mr. Orson wasn't too eager to go back to the table for sandwiches. Turns out, he wasn't in any hurry to return to the escort's line of sight.

Olivia left the balcony, returned to the library, and walked toward Ruth without a word. Not a hint on her face of what kind of trouble Ruth might be in. Olivia passed Ruth, who was now trying to look nonchalant. She leaned casually against the desk, arms crossed in front of her chest, and said, "The third drawer down on the right may hold what you're looking for."

Ruth's eyes went as wide as the saucer her teacup sat on, and then Olivia added, "But there's more to that drawer than appears at first." And with a wink and a smile, Olivia left the room, seeming quite cheerful. Perhaps with a little bounce to her step.

Ruth opened the drawer that Olivia had indicated. It held a pad of blank stationery, envelopes, an extra pen, and unopened ink. But Olivia had said that the drawer was more than it seemed, and Ruth was indeed very clever. She noticed a small lip at the back of the drawer bottom. Lifting at the small lip in the back, Ruth discovered that the drawer had a false bottom. Underneath laid her father's missing ledgers. Of course, Ruth had a few words forming on her lips, but they would have to wait. She slipped the ledgers into the pocket of an apron she had worn under another apron, a sort of false drawer of her own. Then she went back to the bay window to sit in the seat where Claire could see her and grabbed a sandwich. She took a couple of bites before Claire noticed with great relief that she was back. Ruth nodded slightly, grinning.

"Shall we have a sandwich, Mr. Orson, before the seagulls fly away with them?" Claire joked with the man.

Olivia had cut the sandwiches into lovely little triangles and removed the crust. They did look delicious, but Claire barely managed to eat one because of Mr. Orson's repulsive lip-smacking noises as well as nerves. Now came the next stage of her plan, probably the riskier part of her plan. Gathering her resolve, she then suggested that they should probably go back in and return to help with the market, bracing herself for what she had to do next. Mr. Orson was concerned that they hadn't had a chance to have pie, and Claire assured him that it was quite alright, suggesting he could enjoy the pie at his night's end as he contemplated his day.

Once back inside the library, Claire stopped intentionally to admire the velvet shoe once more, steadying herself internally. "It really is an amazing piece, Mr. Orson. Just imagine if you were to have the mate to that shoe. Think of what it would be worth to have the set," she tempted.

"More than all I own, to be sure. But that is impossible. But; what I wouldn't give to own that other shoe. That would be my greatest treasure. That would be *the* greatest treasure. Wouldn't I be the envy then?" He imagined.

Claire let him envision his greatness a moment before she baited, "What if I told you that it wasn't impossible, Mr. Orson?"

"What are you talking about, Claire?" Mr. Orson snapped, his red nostrils flaring.

"Would you be willing to bargain with me, if I told you I could give you the other shoe?" she asked. Her knees were weak, and her heart was racing, unsure of what this greedy man would do. This was it, the point of no return. Ruth was literally on her toes, poised for whatever might happen next.

"Do not toy with me girl, what are you playing at?" He was becoming quite agitated at this point, not daring to believe that this mere girl, washed in from the sea with nothing to her name could possibly be a key to the mate of this most prized treasure. "Make your point, and quickly, I tire of your game," not used to being the one who didn't have the upper hand, knowing instinctively that Claire was not bluffing.

Claire reached into the pocket of the apron she too had worn under another apron producing the shoe. Mr. Orson's face went whiter than it already was so as to look almost blue. He stumbled back half a step before lunging forward towards Claire, grabbing for the shoe. Claire screamed involuntarily and jumped out of the way. Ruth was at Claire's side in an instant. Her hands balled up in tiny fists.

"Get back Mr. Orson or I swear…" Brave little Ruth warned him.

Mr. Orson regained himself, straightened out his suit jacket and the fishtail handkerchief in the breast pocket of his expensive suit, "Where did you? How…" was all he could whisper.

Olivia came in the library door, "Is everything all right? I heard an, um, a noise."

"Thank you, Olivia, we're all right. But would you mind staying, as a witness?" Claire asked, containing herself.

Mr. Orson glared venomously at Claire, then at Olivia.

Olivia answered with a certain resolution, "Yes ma'am." Quick to agree because she had been listening outside the door like all good housemaids.

"Mr. Orson, I would gladly hand you this shoe at no cost," Claire informed him. A wave of confidence suddenly ran through her as she added, "I want only one thing from you. You will leave the Harrington family alone. You will no longer badger them about their property. You will leave Mr. Harrington alone and return his ledgers."

At this, he interrupted, "I have no idea what you're talking about. I don't have his ledgers. Why would I have his ledgers?"

Ruth took the ledgers out of her pocket, and Mr. Orson jabbed forward to grab them.

"Why you little…" he started as Olivia cleared her throat loudly, stopping him from any further movement or commentary.

"As I was saying, we get the ledgers and you leave the family alone." Claire finished.

"Oh, and one last thing," she added, "I'll write up a note stating our agreement for you to sign, and Olivia will sign as a witness. Not another word will be said of this from either side."

"Mr. Spencer will sign also, you'll need two witnesses." Olivia proclaimed, attempting in futility to conceal her grin.

Ruth and Claire left the town's bank and import-export business and walked back towards the Harrington's wagon. At first, not saying a word to each other, they just kept looking at one another and back to Mr. Orson's. Their faces hurt from holding the giant grins. Far enough away from Mr. Orson's establishment to feel safe, they had to stop in the middle of the street to burst out laughing, partly from exhilaration, mostly from relief.

"Ruth, you are the most amazing person I know!" Claire told her after regaining herself and hugging the young girl.

"Well, really Claire, you don't know very many people," Ruth replied, throwing them both into another fit of laughter as they continued down the street.

Claire and Ruth walked up to Helen, who was looking at them suspiciously.

"Don't you two look like the cat that ate the canary? What have you been up to? What took you so long?" Helen asked.

The girls just smiled and shrugged.

Claire directed, "Ruthie, why don't you go find your dad and Kyle and bring them back here. Then we can explain it to everybody at the same time. Don't show them what you've got until we're all together, okay?"

"Okay, Mom?" Ruth asked with such obvious excitement Helen could only agree. She looked at Ruth and then at Claire. Seeing that they weren't going to offer an explanation until they were all together she said, "Go on then, hurry."

Claire gave Helen a lingering hug then went and sat in the front of the wagon. From there, she could see out to the water. She sat there basking in their moment of triumph, still trying to believe what she and Ruth had just done, grateful beyond words that they were okay. A disturbance coming from the docks drew her attention. Two seagulls were squawking and pecking at each other, fighting over something. Squinting out towards the water's edge, her hand shielding her eyes, she could finally make out what the silly birds were fussing over. It looked like a wig, a tall white wig. Only it wasn't so tall or white anymore. It had washed up on shore, covered in silt and tangled with seaweed. Those poor birds were fighting over it like they had found the greatest treasure. Claire laughed out loud. *What do they see in that silly wig?'* she thought.

The family gathered; Ruth and Claire recounted their story. With Ruth adding zest and flavor to the tale, both the girls barreled through their account, hardly believing it themselves as they unfolded the events. Wrapping up the details, Ruth presented Robert with the ledgers. Claire produced the letter signed by Mr. Orson and the witnesses. Helen, Robert, and Kyle just stared at the two girls, shocked and amazed until the girls began to think that they were in trouble, their hearts sinking. Seeing their discomfort, Robert snapped out of his disbelief first and laughed. He laughed the loud, throw your head back laugh, brings tears to your eyes laugh of a man who just had the weight of the world lifted off his shoulders. This brought Helen around and she took both the girls in her arms and cried her own tears of relief, and told them about five times how proud she was of them. Kyle just grinned, shaking his head.

"So it was you Claire; our amazing gift from the sea. You were the answer I couldn't quite see." Robert exclaimed as he took his turn embracing the girls.

15

INCREDIBLY, MR. ORSON kept his word. He even acted pleasantly surprised when Robert presented him with his copies of the supposedly missing ledgers, even though they both knew the whole truth. Mr. Orson had to save face after all, and Robert did not have a problem with letting him hold onto his false pride. After all, it didn't matter to Robert. He wasn't expecting, nor did he need an apology. Robert had his family, and they were going to be alright. Mr. Orson could sit in his library with his so-called treasures. It was a lucky man who knew the worth of the truest treasure. Robert considered himself a very lucky man.

Olivia and Bart Spencer were just leaving the Harrington's house as the sun was setting on a late summer evening. They had wanted to visit the family and share their good news. After the incident at Mr. Orson's, Claire and Ruth's bravery helped them both finally make the decision they couldn't bring themselves to make before.

They were both quite unhappy in the employment of Mr. Orson. It often happens that when you spend too much time in the company of a person who is truly miserable themselves this miserable person will pull you down with them. Mr. Orson was always very demeaning to both Olivia and poor Mr. Spencer, telling them that they were lucky he was so patient with them and they would never be employable anywhere else because nobody else would be as patient as he and other such nasty untruths. They had heard it all so often that they started to believe it. Olivia and Bart had had feelings for each other for quite some time, but neither had the confidence to let the other know. Bart felt unworthy of Olivia, so beautiful and funny. He was worried that he could never provide for her in the manner he felt he should and Olivia couldn't imagine what such a dignified man like Bart would ever see in a maid.

When they saw those two girls stand up to Mr. Orson they were able to see him in a new way. His narcissistic ways began to seem silly. Olivia would often have to hold back a giggle. Bart gathered up his courage one day and asked Olivia if she would consider joining him on a stroll through the street market. They laughed and talked the whole afternoon. In fact, they were both late in returning to Mr. Orson's, who huffed his displeasure at both of them. Bart and Olivia just looked at each other and laughed. Poor Mr. Orson didn't know what to do; many of the things he held true were falling apart. After that, Bart and Olivia spent every moment together that propriety would allow. Mr. Spencer wasted no time proposing to his beloved treasure, Olivia. They had come to see the

Harrington's to tell them that they had both quit their jobs with Mr. Orson. After they were married the following week, they moved to the big city where Bart was going to work for an up-and-coming accounting firm.

Robert and Helen decided to walk with Olivia and Bart for a while towards Olivia's. Helen and Olivia discussed their simple wedding plans while Robert and Burt commiserated about the possibility of Burt taking over the Harrington's accounts. Robert had plans for expanding his business.

The night was lovely, just reaching twilight. Ruth, Kyle, and Claire sat out on the front porch, watching the moon, full and bright, slowly trading places with the sun. The last traces of pink were settling behind the water's edge.

Kyle, although just on the top step of the porch seemed miles away, while Claire and Ruth sat on the porch swing, swinging slightly, lost in their own thoughts. A little bat fluttered by doing its aerial acrobatics, feasting thankfully on mosquitoes and other pesky bugs, bringing Kyle back from his preoccupation. He turned to look at Claire, who returned his gaze wondering why he looked so serious.

"Claire, can I talk to you for a minute?" he asked, holding out his hand.

"Sure," Claire responded, rising from the swing and attempting to take his hand.

At Ruth's knowing grin, Kyle became self-conscious and dropped his hand, placing it in his pocket. He then indicated with a tilt of his head over his shoulder for Claire to follow him.

"We'll be right back, Ruth." He told her.

"Okay," Ruth replied with that smile still sitting on her face, "I'm just going to head on up to bed."

Kyle led Claire along the property across the grass, stopping about thirty paces from the cliff's edge. Claire came up to stand to the right of Kyle, looking out to the sea below. The upper parts of the evergreen trees growing on the cliff sides peaked over to the left and right. Down to the left, beyond that you could see a rocky shore jutting out, waves crashing against the rocks.

"This is my favorite spot." Kyle told Claire, "You can hear the waves hitting the rocks. Listen."

Claire closed her eyes and listened; there was a soft, soothing, powerful rhythm.

Kyle continued, "When I'm all done with my chores sometimes or after supper, I like to come here and lie in the grass and listen. I usually fall asleep." he confessed, "Or I'll sit at the edge of the cliff there and think. "

Claire looked startled at this idea, and Kyle explained that the cliff didn't drop off like it looked. There was a trail on the left side where you could climb down boulders and get to a small beach, and he would take her there sometime. Then he continued, "One afternoon, right here where we're standing, I fell asleep. It was nice. The sun was warm, and the grass smelled sweet. I could hear the waves breaking; before I knew it, I was dreaming. That was when I had that dream, you know, the one I told you about? When we were fishing?" he searched her face anxiously to see if she remembered. Of course, she remembered.

He was quiet for a moment then looked down, taking both Claire's hands in his. Claire felt a rush of heat flowing from her fingertips through her entire being, flushing her face, stopping her heart for a beat, and causing a catch in her breath. Kyle blew out a long mouthful of air; he had been holding his breath. He then opened his hands, palms up. Claire kept her hands on his, palms down, her eyes going from their hands to Kyle's face or rather the top of his head. He was still staring at their hands as he pulled his arms back slightly so that their fingertips were just touching. He caressed Claire's fingertips with his thumbs as he thought about how to continue. Claire would have been happy to stand there all night this way. His hands were warm, his fingers long. They were working hands strong and slightly rough, but they held hers so gently. Finally, Kyle slid his hands back to hold Claire's again. He looked up, Claire's eyes followed, and he started after clearing his throat, "I didn't tell you the whole story Claire; I'd like to tell you now if that's okay."

He looked at her with such vulnerability. She could see that he was scared, and she wasn't so sure that she wanted to hear this. She looked back down at their hands. His hold was still so gentle, she felt reassured and said simply, "Alright," looking up to his solemn face again.

"I didn't just hear your name as I said. I saw you. I saw *you,* Claire, as plain as you are standing here. I was on the shore, and you were walking out of the sea towards me. You were so beautiful, you *are* so beautiful. And you're kind and talented. You have great gifts, Claire. Even in my dream, I knew these things about you." At this, Claire made a sound of disbelief.

"You don't think so?" Kyle asked.

"No… I mean… I can make a good pie, but what is that compared to the gifts you and your family have? I have a couple of talents but I don't think I have any special gifts," she answered.

"I know you do. Gifts aren't always obvious," Kyle said and Claire rolled her eyes, turning her head away.

Kyle put his fingers to her chin, turned her head to look at him, and said earnestly, "You are really new to this world in many ways, Claire. Your gifts will show themselves in time. And they'll be great, I know it."

When Claire did not argue, he continued, "Before Dad left for his last voyage, he told me I needed to work as much as I could and start saving my money. He gave me strict instructions to put it away, save as much as I could, and when the time came, I would know what it was for. Kyle laughed a small laugh, mostly to himself, "Claire, when I pulled you from the water, I couldn't believe my eyes. I couldn't believe it was you, the face I had seen in my dream. Then you told me your name! I still didn't want to trust my dream."

He looked back out at the sea and sighed. A seagull called from somewhere far off then all was quiet again so that you could hear the waves on the rocks below. A small peaceful smile appeared on Kyle's face, his eyes were closed. With that smile on his face, he looked back at Claire and finished, "I'd like to build a house, right here. I'd like to build a home." And he paused, "For you and me, Claire."

Kyle stopped, trying to figure out what Claire was thinking, what that look on her face meant. Shock? Her eyes were pretty big. Had he just ruined everything? Too late now, it was already said. He loved her, he had to go forward.

"I'm in love with you, Claire. I have been since before I met you. Would you consider having a home with me? Here? Could you possibly consider marrying me?" Kyle searched her face for an answer for what seemed an eternity, and then Claire smiled and shocked Kyle, as well as herself, by putting a hand gently on his face, her palm on his cheek. Kyle flushed and put his hand atop hers as if to lock it there. He didn't care how his heart was racing.

She stared at this young man in front of her. He looked so sure of what he was saying, but there was pleading in his eyes. There was that kind and handsome face she had seen on the shore. He had saved her life then and was offering it to her again now.

Once again, she saw in her mind the little red fish with the funny white wigs. They were swimming in circles when a cloud of bubbles rose from below, startling them. They swam quickly away, and Claire couldn't see them anymore. Up through the bubbles rose a woman. Her skin was a silvery green; her long hair flowed out around her moving sinuously with the water's currents. Fish were swimming in and out of her curls. Her face was wild and beautiful with large round eyes. They were completely glassy silver with a slit of a metallic black pupil, not a bit of white. She smiled with a mouth slightly too wide for her face exposing a row of sharp teeth. Claire noticed this woman holding a large ship in one delicately webbed hand. The woman spoke to Claire in a watery voice saying simply, "Welcome home," as the vision faded.

Claire stepped closer to Kyle and leaning in, gave him one gentle lingering kiss on his lips, warm, sweet and soft. Now it was Kyle's turn to go spinny. His heart skipped a beat and his breath caught in his throat as Claire pulled slowly away leaving his lips tingling and wanting hers back on his just as he had been wanting guiltily since he had put his lips to hers to save her.

Claire sighed contentedly and said, "I'm in love with you too, Kyle Harrington. Yes."

Part Two

1

KYLE WANTED TO WAIT until the house was built before he and Claire were married. He wanted to have a home of their own to offer his bride, a threshold of their own to carry her over. Claire agreed to this on one condition: it just had to be livable, not 'finished' in the sense that Kyle would consider finished. With Kyle's eye for detail and the care he put into the trinket and jewelry boxes he crafted as well as the brush sets (they were absolutely beautiful), Claire figured he would put just as much thought into the finished work of their home. She was right; Kyle had a lot of plans.

Kyle and his father Robert would be able to work on the house steady through the summer. Robert's last trip out to sea for goods, before the debacle over the ledgers, was quite profitable. He could thus afford to stay home awhile. Kyle had saved a good sum of money over the last couple of years as his father had suggested, allowing him to purchase what was needed to build their home. They milled some lumber from the family's property but not too much, it wasn't a heavily wooded area. They didn't want to deplete it in any way, so they bought a good portion of the wood from the mill. Kyle's mother Helen, his sister Ruth and Claire all put in their sweat equity too.

The Harrington family continued to sell at the street market through the summer. Helen sold her quilts, nightgowns, and other things she decided to sew and embellish with her sought-after embroidery work. They also had their goat cheese, jellies, pies, Kyle's jewelry boxes, and other woodwork items. Claire wanted to help out more than she was with the building and furnishing of the house and the Harrington family's needs in general, so she was able to get a job at the bakery a couple of days a week.

Mary, the bakery owner, was more than happy to have Claire's help. Claire's pies were becoming quite famous at the street market. Mary had to admit that Claire's pies were better than hers. The bakery was excellent before, but on the days Claire worked, people would have to sit outside to eat because there wasn't enough room inside. Mary ordered an awning and set out extra tables and chairs on the boardwalk to accommodate the overflow. It wasn't just because of Claire's pies. Claire was well-loved. She had a warmth about her that people responded to. People felt at ease immediately in her presence. Claire found that she would often know a person's whole life story by the time they left. Not that she would ever pry, they would just start telling her and they would inevitably apologize, claiming they didn't know what came over them. Still, Claire was always gracious, insisting that no apology was necessary.

Summer was moving along and so was the house. Kyle and Claire had decided to set the house in line, but further back from the parent's home. Their living room window would face the cliffs, overlooking the sea where Kyle and Claire had proclaimed their love, but would not impair the elder Harrington's view. The outhouse and washroom were built out from the back of the home. They decided to expand and work on the existing garden instead of plotting another.

Robert had sent a telegraph to some of his ship's crew members and sent word out around town that they were ready to raise the walls on Kyle and Claire's house. On the days decided, over a dozen people showed up in answer to his call for help. People slept in the barn and under the stars. Helen, Ruth, and Claire, along with a couple of wives who came along, were kept busy cooking breakfast, dinner, and supper for the house-raising crew; keeping them filled with rabbit and venison stews, casserole bread, and pies and they kept the lavender mint cold tea flowing. On the last night, when all the work was done, they had a feast of venison roast, turkey, fish, and fresh corn on the cob, as well as tomatoes and zucchini from the garden.

The street market was now closed, and it was getting about time to pull in the last harvests. The corn was at its end, and the squash and zucchini were done. The little green pumpkins were getting bigger; they would start turning color within a few weeks. The nights were cooling down, and the days were getting a little shorter every week. Robert and Kyle had already helped Mr. Marshall bring in his hay for this season. You could see the color on the trees starting to turn. It was sad to see the summer end, but that also meant that fall was coming. Helen loved the fall and winter. People would put down their plows and pick up their needle points. It was the season for mending and sitting by the fire, telling stories.

Kyle started some projects for the new house down at the barn and Claire wasn't allowed to peek. He wanted to surprise her. On many nights, after dinner and chores, Kyle would disappear down to the barn working by lantern light deep into the night. Claire was dying to know what he was up to down there, but he was so cute about it that she couldn't bring herself to steal a look. Plus, Ruth was under strict orders to 'keep an eye on her'. Minnie the goat and Rose the family milk cow were happy for the company and were sworn to secrecy too.

Fall was officially brought in by the community with the Annual Harvest Social. It was always an anticipated event held partly at the church. The gentleman who owned the hardware and feed store set up a giant three-sided tent under which the mill owner built a big dance floor and stage. There was inevitably an impromptu band made up of the talents of the people within the community. The church pews would be hauled out on the beach so people could sit around the bonfires. In their place, long tables covered with all types of foods provided by the attendees would fill the chapel. It was a very 'kick back have fun after all your hard work with the harvest' party.

Helen, Ruth, and Claire were putting together a sweet potato dish and baking up half a dozen loaves of zucchini bread. Robert and Kyle had been busy all week catching and smoking as much fish as they could.

As it was getting time to head down to town for the social, Claire was getting nervous. She knew most of the people by now and her job at the bakery had helped her become more comfortable with meeting new people. What made her most nervous was the fact that there was going to be dancing. As far as she knew, she had no idea how to dance.

There was still so much that she didn't know. Everything was gone from memory before Kyle had saved her life, bringing her in from the sea where she had been drowning, except for occasional odd glimpses of a girl she didn't recognize but felt must be her. There were strange little red fish and lots of water, although she hadn't had a 'memory' in quite some time. She didn't worry about her life before, she was happy and didn't have any desire to be anything or anywhere other than who she was now and what her life was becoming.

"Claire, are you okay tonight?" Ruth asked as they were getting ready for the evening's events. Ruth was a few years younger than Claire but very intuitive. She could read people well, not that Claire was being all that difficult to read right now.

As Claire was helping Ruth take the rags out of her hair (Ruth wanted to keep her hair down and curled like some of the older girls did), Claire asked, "Do you think there will be dancing there?"

"Oh my goodness, Claire!" Ruth exclaimed with her usual fervor, "I've never seen you dance! Do you even know how to dance?"

"I have no idea," Claire answered. "I don't think so."

"MOM!!" Ruth yelled, running out of Claire's room into the kitchen, half the rag curls still tied in, skidding to a stop at her mom's room, knocking loudly at the door, even as Helen was opening it.

"What's the matter, Ruthie?" Helen responded anxiously, looking for signs of blood by the way Ruth had screamed.

"Claire can't dance!" Ruth answered, eyes wide with concern.

"What?" Helen was still recovering from the scare from Ruth's scream, "Claire can't what? Dance?" she continued as she looked over at Claire.

Claire shrugged and they both smiled. Helen placed a hand on Ruth's shoulder, which was almost even with hers now. Ruth had grown and turned into a young lady over the summer, although she was still getting used to the idea as her before-mentioned behavior indicated. "Is that all?" Helen said with relief, "your dad is down at the barn brushing out the horse before we head into town and Kyle is working on his project. Ask them to come up and we'll have a quick lesson."

The men came up and Claire was embarrassed to see the grins on their faces they were trying to hide. Her embarrassment was quickly replaced with surprise when Kyle returned down the stairs from his room with a violin in hand. He began to play as Helen and Robert proceeded to show Claire a few simple steps. She wondered if this young man she was in love with and planned to spend the rest of her life with was ever going to stop amazing her. She doubted it. Ruth then became Claire's dance partner, taking the lead, walking her through the steps. Claire was pleased to find that she took to it quite naturally. She was then passed off to Robert, Kyle changed the tune, and they taught her a couple more steps.

"Okay boys, you need to go get cleaned up and we ladies need to finish making ourselves beautiful," Helen announced as she broke up the dance lesson.

"I don't think it would be fair to the other women at the party if the ladies of the Harrington house were any more beautiful," Kyle responded, kissing his sister on the head, not taking his eyes off Claire, hardly able to believe that he had done anything in his life to be worthy of this woman.

The Harrington family led Sunrise with the wagon to the designated area set aside for the teams of horses. Robert had built another bench in the back of the wagon to accommodate his changing family. With the addition of Claire, and Ruth now a young woman, there had to be better seating. They couldn't sprawl on the wagon floor as Ruth did just a short time ago.

It was just barely supper time and the sun was already setting. The sky was getting dark and the first stars were shining brightly in the twilight. The air was crisp, and bonfires were already crackling on the beach.

The dance floor was lit up with colorful paper lanterns, and torches lit the walkways. The windows in the church were alight and the steps were decorated with pumpkins and gourds sitting on bales of hay, corn stalks tied in bundles, and baskets of apples welcoming everybody in.

The women took the food they had prepared into the church, turned to the dining hall, which was already filled with delicious smells. All the food was just as beautiful to look at as was the inviting aroma. They found a place on one of the tables to lay their fare, and the men helped the other neighbors and friends bring in more chairs and see what else they could do to help. Mary from the bakery had brought over a supply of dishes and silverware for the festivities as well as tablecloths that had already been laid out.

It was time to bless the food and start the party. The minister gathered the people outside the building and offered a prayer of thanksgiving stating their gratitude for blessings and asking for health and safety for their little community. After the last amen, they took turns filling their plates with all the wonderful food provided. Some people sat inside the church at the few tables therein, and many sat outside at the tables provided there and around the perimeter of the dance floor. Wherever they were sitting, the conversation was decidedly hushed since the food was just so good.

As was tradition, everybody washed their own dishes in the church's small kitchen so nobody would have to miss the fun. When it looked like the last of the attendees were finishing up their dishes, one of the men picked up his guitar, took his chair to the outdoor stage, and started playing a quiet song. Soon after, one of the women joined him at the church's piano that had been brought out for the occasion. People started bringing more chairs and standing around the outskirts of the dance floor.

Mr. and Mrs. Warren were the first to grace the dance floor, a sweet older couple that lived down the far end of the beach in one of the last houses down that way. It was one of the township's oldest homes.

Mr. Warren had built it for his wife before she had even met him. He was now a retired fisherman, and when he was a young man, he had gone into the city with his ship's captain to see about setting up some contracts with a couple of the restaurants there; the not-yet Mrs. Warren had caught his eye. She was the daughter of one of the restaurant owners and was waiting tables. He was too shy to introduce himself and felt he smelled of fish but he was determined to marry her right then and there. Mr. Warren worked four years to save money and build their house before he even officially met her. He would arrange to accompany the captain often when they needed to meet with the restaurant owner, hoping to catch a glimpse of her. When he was done with the house and had a respectable amount of money in the bank, he bought a nice suit and went to the restaurant, hoping beyond hope she had not already married or moved away, or that he had lost his chance in any of the many ways he was imagining. But she was there, and she had been waiting for him too.

After Mr. and Mrs. Warren got the dancing started, more people joined the band on the dance floor. Claire, Ruth, and Kyle were occupying one of the tables around the dance floor. Robert and Helen were already dancing. Mr. Orson had arrived. Claire noticed he was looking a little out of place as he hung to the outskirts looking around the crowd. He spotted Claire and gave a little start. She looked stunning, and he flushed a little. He was wearing an immaculately tailored suit with a perfectly positioned pocket hankie as usual. His hair didn't seem to be swept up quite as high in that unusual pouf he normally wore. He noticed that Claire was looking at him too, so he puffed out his chest and decided to go mingle.

Claire reacted very negatively when she first met this man and found she had reason to dislike him. His arrogance and greed had almost cost the Harrington family all they owned. He wanted Claire for himself as well as the Harrington property. He was a wealthy man and had all he needed, living above the town's bank and import-export business he owned. Thanks to Claire and Ruth, his plan to acquire the Harrington's property had failed, and he was slightly humbled. Only slightly. Claire found she could no longer dislike the man but instead had compassion for him.

Robert had been in partnership with Dale, or Mr. Orson, for a long time and knew him well. He understood how lonely Dale was and how blessed he and his family were to have each other, and all Dale had was his so-called treasures he surrounded himself with. Robert and Helen set an example of compassion and tolerance.

Mr. Hansen, the town's grocer, who Claire hadn't realized played the harmonica and quite well at that, jumped from the stage and ran over to Kyle, "You bring that fiddle of yours, Kyle?" he inquired.

"Yes I did sir, it's in the wagon," Kyle replied with a shy grin.

"Well, go get it! We need you up here!" Mr. Hansen replied, shaking Kyle by the shoulder jovially.

Kyle returned with his violin and joined the band. They played some beautiful slow songs and some rip-up-the-floor dancing songs that got everybody clapping and stomping.

Mr. Marshall and his family were in attendance, accompanied by their oldest boy William who had been away to school to become a doctor. His dad was very proud and was parading him around to everybody. William was the first one in the family to go to college, and his dad had every right to be proud. But William was embarrassed and glad to see Ruth and Claire sitting at the table.

Asking if he could join them, he confided beneath his breath, "I feel like my own personal parade." They grinned and offered him a chair.

Ruth was barraging William with questions about school, and he was answering her enthusiastically when Mr. Orson approached.

"Good evening, Claire. Ruth, William." He greeted in his usual lofty tone. "How are things at the university, William?"

"It's going great, thank you. I still have a couple of years there, and then I'll have an internship. But I should be ready to have my own practice in about five years." William answered.

"Yes, and Ruth you look lovely this evening. Are you having a good time?" Mr. Orson inquired with forced interest.

"Thank you, Mr. Orson, yes, it's a lovely evening, and yourself?" was Ruth's cordial response. Claire was proud of Ruth for not telling Mr. Orson to go suck eggs or something. She was turning into a lovely young woman, she thought amusingly to herself.

"Yes, yes, lovely." Mr. Orson returned impatiently as he looked to Claire and asked, "Would you do me the honor of a dance?" as he extended a hand, his other folded behind his back.

Claire took his hand awkwardly, accepting his invitation, thinking she saw relief in his stoic face. They took to the dance floor, Claire going nervously over the dance steps in her head she had learned earlier that night. Much to her surprise, she found herself gliding easily across the dance floor without having to give it much thought. She was a natural dancer and she was equally surprised to find that Mr. Orson was a gracious and graceful dancer himself.

Not knowing where to rest her eyes and not wanting to stare into Mr. Orson's, Claire gazed around the room. They danced by Ruth and William, Ruth raised her eyebrows at her slightly as they sashayed by, making Claire grin to herself. Robert and Helen nodded cordially as they danced by. Afraid she would get the giggles, she dared not look at Kyle. Shortly after they passed the stage though, Robert and Helen danced up beside them and indicated a partner change. Robert took Claire and Helen cheerily took up step with Mr. Orson.

The song came to an end as Robert escorted Claire to her seat and then returned to Helen, who was still visiting with Mr. Orson; Claire joined the conversation with Ruth and William. Feeling a tap on her shoulder, she turned to see Kyle, slightly bent at the waist, right hand extended. There was that grin she couldn't resist as he asked, "May I have this dance?"

Kyle brought his left hand around, placing it gently on the small of her back, pulling Claire towards him slightly as she placed her right hand lightly on his shoulder. With Claire's left hand in Kyle's right, they stood motionless for the smallest of seconds. Claire's breath caught then quickened, feeling the warmth of his hand on her back. Kyle flushed a bit as he caught a wisp of her scent – she smelt of honey and berries. He noticed pleasantly that his hand fit perfectly across the small of her back. This was their first dance. Claire couldn't take her eyes off of his; they danced, unaware of anybody around them.

They danced right through two songs before they came out of their spell, a little embarrassed by the knowing smiles from the older couples remembering their brand-new loves. Claire and Kyle walked to the bonfire on the beach to relieve their embarrassment and get away from the knowing smiles. Claire could see Mr. Orson walking towards town, heading home, alone.

2

R UTH SAT ON THE END of Claire's bed, talking excitedly as Claire finished her packing. "I've only been on the train once and was too young to remember. I hope we'll have time to see the university while we're in the city. I wonder if William will be available, he said the school has a great veterinary program. Oh Claire, do you think I really could go to college? Do you think I really could be a veterinarian? That would be so amazing! William says there are only two women in the program and one of them is one of the professors. A woman professor! Actually, she studied nursing first, then as a veterinarian. Oh, be sure to pack your gloves and hat, oh, and a scarf, it's getting so cold out. Have you noticed?"

The Harrington family was packing for a two-day trip to the city. Helen wanted to buy fabric for the wedding dress she was making Claire as well as other supplies. The men had a few things planned too; Kyle needed to pick up a suit for one thing. They had sent a letter to Olivia and Bart Spencer who were now residing in the city asking if they could recommend a place to stay. The Spencers returned their letter with an enthusiastic "Yes! With us! We have an extra room for the girls and we have arranged for the men to stay with a neighbor!"

With a friend taking care of the animals, the Harrington family was on their way. Mr. Marshall gave them all a ride into town to the stables where they chartered a wagon to the train station. The stables had a fancy two-horse wagon with cushioned bench seats facing each other and a flatbed in the back for luggage. There was a canvas cover over the top of the whole thing to keep the sun off the passengers, with sides that could roll down to keep out the weather when needed. It would be an hour's ride by wagon to the train station and another one-and-a-half-hour train ride into the city.

Once on the train, Robert ordered sweet biscuits and sarsaparillas for the family from the dining car. He had splurged and paid for a private compartment with extra soft seats, pillows, and blankets. Helen, Robert, and Kyle all fell asleep for the last leg of the ride, but Claire and Ruth were too excited and didn't want to miss a thing. The other three had made this trip a few times, but it was all new to the girls. They marveled at the speed at which the trees were shooting past. Claire was intrigued by the base rhythm that chugga-chugged as the train shot along the tracks, accompanied by the various creaks, tinkles, and clankity-clanks from the train and low rumbling voices of its occupants. She could feel a tune teasing at the edge of her mind.

The whistle blew, announcing the train's arrival at the station at the lip of the city. The brakes screeched and squealed startlingly, causing Claire to grab her seat while Ruth grabbed on to Claire; they had never heard such a disturbing commotion.

The family couldn't help but giggle at the girls, their eyes as big as saucers due to the unnatural clamor. Ruth and Claire saw their expressions mirrored in each other's face and had to laugh too.

Robert kissed his daughter on the top of the head and said, "Alright, the train is right on time; Olivia and Bart are probably looking for us. Let's grab our luggage."

Sure enough, they found the Spencers, Olivia waving madly, not too far down the dock. Bart took some of the luggage, and the women all exchanged heartfelt hugs, the men offered hearty handshakes, and they led them through the busy platform towards the street.

Olivia and Bart had never looked better. They had been so unhappy back home, both employees for Mr. Orson who was a bear to work for, to say the least. Then they had gained the courage from Ruth and Claire's example to stand up for themselves and quit. Olivia and Bart also gained the courage to let each other know how they had felt about each other for so long. Now they were married and living in the city, a life that obviously agreed with both of them. Olivia wore a casual but very smart-looking dress in what must have been a new style. It was more fitted than what they were wearing back home. Helen was excited to look around some of the shops and see what the women in the city were wearing. She could incorporate some of these new ideas into her sewing. Bart's suit wasn't such a surprise due to Mr. Orson's example back home, being aware of what was considered the height of men's fashion, but the fabric was interesting. It seemed durable but still had a silky sheen that striped through it. On Bart, the cut of the suit seemed less stuffy than it would on poor Mr. Orson.

Outside the station waiting for the group was an elegant horse-drawn coach. This coach was completely enclosed with a beautifully polished wood cab with sheer curtained windows. It had brass railings on the very top that held the luggage. Brass steps led inside to rich leather seats; there was even floral wallpaper lining the interior. Outside the carriage, the driver sat up high, almost even with the top of the carriage so that through the front window, all you could see was his gleaming boots. His seat was held aloft with spiraled brass workings that acted as springs. There were similar springs under the whole carriage to ensure a comfortable ride. The coach offered a trundle seat on the back where Kyle and Bart sat. The horses pulling the carriage were beautiful and well cared for. Their mane and tail were braided with red ribbons and orange glass beads. Their coats were washed and brushed to gleaming. When the family was settled, they pulled a fine gold rope that rang a small bell next to the driver, indicating they were ready to go.

The horses' hooves tapped out a pleasing rhythm as the dirt road turned to cobblestone when they approached the city.

Claire was almost overwhelmed by the smells as the group got closer to the populated little metropolis. Not all the smells were pleasant. There was an odor of fires from the many stoves, food being prepared in a dozen different ways. She could smell the musk of horses, and the ever-underlying stink from garbage and the waste created by that many people living so closely together. She was unaware that she had wrinkled up her nose as Olivia assured her, "Doesn't smell quite like home, does it?" With a reassuring grin and touch to Claire's knee she added, "You get used to it, well, mostly."

Bart and Olivia lived right in the city proper in a four-story brick apartment building. The coach pulled up to the front of the building along the sidewalk. Four wide concrete steps led up to heavy wood double doors. The apartment building was even taller than the three-story building Mr. Orson owned and resided in.

As they entered the building, there was a hall to the left and stairs to the right. Olivia gave the 'tour' and explained as they went, "This is the first floor. Down that hall there, see the doors? There are four privies, one for each floor. Each door is marked number one for everybody that lives on floor one, two for two, and so on. Each floor has its own bathroom down here. Inside! Can you believe it? So up we go!" She continued as she led them on.

"We are on the second floor. Good thing too, because it's not as far from the bathrooms as floor four, but not as close as one!" And she laughed at her joke.

On the second floor now, the stairs continued up on the right with the halls to their left. "There are three apartments to each floor," she explained as they walked down the second-floor hall. "As you can see, there are two on the right and one on the left, due to the stairs you know. Here we are! Last room on the left! Apartment 2a. That's us!" And as she ushered them inside their apartment with apparent pride, she added, "Home sweet home!"

The Spencers apartment was good sized for a city apartment. They were fairly new and came with an icebox and two burner wood stove. The wood stove was smaller than the Harrington's, but a good size for apartment living. Olivia informed them that they didn't do a lot of cooking in the summer. The stove cooked them right out of the apartment. There were two bedrooms to the back of the apartment. The bigger bedrooms had a door leading to a small patio facing the alley. The smaller two had a nice sized window that also opened to the alley. The apartments to the front of the building had a patio off the front of the living room above the sidewalks and a window at the street side of the kitchen. All apartments had a window at the side of the living room, outside of which were clotheslines on a pulley system attached to the building next to it.

After they had a moment to settle in and use the facilities, Olivia served them sandwiches that she reported with apparent affection Bart had prepared earlier because he makes 'The best egg salad'. Then the men went over to meet Mr. Poddensky, their host for the weekend.

Mr. Poddensky was a crotchety old gentleman that lived alone in his one-bedroom apartment across the hall from the Spencer's. He was in reality a very kind old man that had taken a liking to Bart and Olivia and was happy for the company. Olivia brought him dinner at least once a week, and Bart always invited him along for Saturday outings, which Mr. Poddensky eventually started accepting.

"Well, don't expect luxury. You'll have to make do with the floor." He grumbled as Bart introduced Robert and Kyle. Bart was staying in the old neighbor's apartment too. In the other apartment, Olivia gave Helen and Ruth the room with the big bed and took up the couch in the living room. There was a cot in the extra room for Claire that a friend had let them borrow.

That night the Spencers took the Harrington family to dinner at the local dinner theater, Olivia and Bart being friends with the owners of the restaurant as well as the actors. They were placed at one of the best seats in the house and treated like royalty the entire evening. They stayed after closing and visited with the theater group, talking about art and theater, trading and faraway places, fashion, and schooling. Finally,

Robert had to excuse the family with great appreciation for such an enjoyable evening; they had a big day ahead of them and had to get an early start.

3

EVERYBODY FOUND WHAT they needed in the city and then some. Ruth was able to tour the school with William and it cemented her determination to attend. Helen found the perfect fabrics and picked up some new tailoring techniques. Robert and Kyle came back with some secret plans up their sleeves. Overall it was an amazing experience, but they were all glad to be back home with the sounds and smells of the ocean at their front door.

The city was fascinating and busy, loud and filled with smells and sound. Many sidewalks were torn up and buildings shut off as more and more indoor plumbing was being brought in. The systems were very similar to what Robert had devised for their own home. There were power lines running electricity to the shops and homes, bringing light with a flip of a switch! Accommodations for telephone lines were coming very soon! It was all so exciting and held so much promise. Imagine being able to pick up a device and speak to somebody miles away like they were right in the room with you. This was an amazing time to be living in. The big cities would see these improvements first, but electricity and telephones were going to make their way to the small towns eventually. It was a slow and expensive process.

Not even home a full day, Kyle and Robert set to work on the new house. The women were informed that none of them were allowed in that area until further notice. They were digging out dirt and hauling it from inside the house. As far as the women knew, the plumbing for the kitchen tap had already been done. The root cellar under the back porch had already been put in and reinforced, the woman had helped haul the rocks and stir the mortar for the cellar walls. The outhouse and drainage for the bathhouse were done too. All these things were done in the summer before the wall raising. But the men weren't giving anything away. The women would have to wait. On top of that undisclosed project, Kyle was still working into the night down at the barn on his other secret endeavors. That was fine with Helen; she had a lot of work to do on Claire's gown as well as Ruth's dress for the wedding, and it wouldn't do to have Kyle see any of that before the nuptials.

The Harringtons worked on the new home and other winter chores through the winter season. Helen and the girls saw to the mending and more sewing. Claire learned how to put up the goat milk soap and hang herbs to dry. Robert and Kyle successfully hunted deer, and the family worked together to get it canned.

The family celebrated Christmas and went to a midnight mass, Mrs. Lawrence sitting in the pew behind them. Mrs. Lawrence often sat behind the Harrington family at church. Claire admired this plucky older woman.

Mrs. Lawrence had been widowed the year before Claire had arrived in this little town along the sea. Helen and Claire brought her treats and a visit at least once a month to her home on the beach. She and her husband had built their home together and raised their children there. The windows were lined with shelves, filled with glass bottles and trinkets catching the sun, throwing shimmering lights of every color around the quaint home.

At first, Claire was quite uncomfortable with these visits. She never knew what to say or do. The home smelled a little of must and fish. But with time, she looked forward to the visits, getting past her original repulsion and feelings of boredom and awkwardness. But it was at church that Mrs. Lawrence unknowingly helped Claire discover another aspect of herself, hidden behind the watery veil.

During the singing of hymns, Claire would sit quietly, reading along and listening. She longed to sing along. The hymns were beautiful and the congregation elicited a feeling of peace and camaraderie when they joined their voices in musical praise. But Claire was self-conscious, not knowing the words and she couldn't remember ever singing.

As she learned the words and became more comfortable with the tune, she began to hum along but couldn't bring herself to sing, afraid she would offend.

One Sunday, as she was listening to the congregation, wishing she could bring herself to sing along, to give praise in song, she heard a single voice behind her, as if all the other voices were miles away. Above them all, she could hear Mrs. Lawrence singing at the top of her lungs, fervently and with such joy. Completely off-key. Yet her song was so filled with joy and praise that Claire had to smile and she too joined the congregation. Timidly at first but soon with confidence. She found that she had a decent voice, but through Mrs. Lawrence's unintended example, it didn't really matter.

Early spring arrived quickly with everybody being so busy with their projects over the winter. The Harringtons had one more surprise in store for Claire. On returning home from the bakery one evening, she was greeted with the yell of "SURPRISE!" as she entered the house. Helen had baked Claire her favorite things for dinner and Ruth had made her carrot cake muffins. There were gifts on the table; Claire was a little confused, to say the least.

Robert explained, "Since we have no idea when your real birthday is, we decided to celebrate it on the day you came into our lives."

They ate dinner and talked about how much had happened since Kyle carried Claire's limp, waterlogged body into the house. After all this time, Claire had never really heard their version of that night. She knew, but it hadn't dawned on her that Kyle had carried her that whole distance from the shore in town to their home up the hill. She learned how Helen and Ruth had been up all night drying Claire's wet matted hair and wrapping her in blankets that they kept warming by the stove until Claire finally stopped shivering. She hadn't realized that she had slept fitfully, coming close to consciousness and out again. They kept a constant watch for three days, trying to get her to sip warm licorice root tea and broth. Finally, on the third night, she slept quietly and woke up on the fourth day.

Claire was again without words for the gratitude she felt and had become quiet as she was fighting back her tears.

"Well, that's enough of that. Here we all are, and grateful for it. Open your gifts now, here's one from Robert and me." Helen declared as she too wiped away her tears, adding lightly, "You know Claire, you're pretty lucky not to know when you were actually born. You don't have all those years hanging over your head!"

"I really do have a child bride!" Kyle teased. "It's almost indecent!"

"Kyle!" His mother unconvincingly scolded. But they all laughed, it was the break they needed. With that, Claire opened her gifts from the family. Robert and Helen gifted her a new pair of shoes to go with her wedding dress. Helen had wrapped them individually in kitchen towels she had embroidered, then wrapped them again in a quilt for their marriage bed. Ruth got her a muffin pan, all the little muffin cups were shaped like mini pumpkins.

"For your own kitchen," Ruth explained proudly. This she had wrapped in pillowcases that Ruth herself had done the needlework on. Ruth was apologetic for the novice stitching, but Claire assured her she would treasure them always.

Finally, Kyle brought out his gift for Claire. It had been tucked away behind the sofa. Luckily Claire had been so touched by the events of the evening (and the family had kept to the kitchen) that she hadn't taken notice that the couch was halfway out into the living room. Kyle brought from behind the sofa a beautiful chest he had made. It had a domed lid with leather strap hinges and a brass clasp. Kyle had engraved the domed lid with intricate blackberries and vines. There was a delicate dragonfly – its wings so elaborately carved you could see all the individual veins – alighted on a blackberry leaf. Claire couldn't believe that Kyle had remembered. Claire had mentioned to Kyle over the summer how she had watched a dragonfly eating a blackberry and how it wasn't afraid. It just sat there eating while Claire got closer and closer to watch. It was an amazing moment for her, and he remembered it. She placed all her gifts reverently inside the chest.

"But wait, there's more!" Kyle exclaimed excitedly as he took her hand and led her to the door.

The family followed as they went down the front porch steps, across the grass to the far side of Claire and Kyle's almost finished house. Claire stretched her neck, trying to get a peek inside the windows, but the night was just turning to dusk and the darkened home wasn't giving away any of its secrets.

"No, you don't," Kyle chided, "just on the other side of the house," he led the procession.

There at the far end of the front porch, so Claire could see the ocean through the clearing above the cliffs, Kyle had built a raised bed for her herb garden. The soil was dark and rich and Claire could smell that it had already been fertilized and treated with the nourishing compost. Kyle reached down beside it and handed Claire a basket filled with little bags, marked with the names of the different seeds for the herbs therein. Thyme, sweet basil, rosemary, and bay to name a few, some with names Claire did not recognize.

It had been a marvelous night, her first birthday, she teased herself as she drifted off to sleep, dreaming of a dark-haired girl wearing an extravagant billowy dress. Beside the dark-haired girl, with curly strands escaping pins and ribbons valiantly trying to hold the complicated twists, sat a man and a woman who so obviously adored this little girl. They were in a room richly decorated with art in large ornate golden frames, silver pieces adorning shelves, and a large crystal chandelier. The heavy open drapes flanked very tall oversized windows that spilt light across velvety overstuffed chairs and couches. In the center of the room, placed before the girl, was a short table overflowing with elaborately wrapped gifts. The image was bright at first, but only for that moment in dreams that could last less than a hummingbird's heartbeat or perhaps it was hours that she stared, before it became cloudy and began to fade as Claire realized that the girl was not elated as one would think, rather, she seemed bored. Claire woke uneasily, sad for that girl. She went to the end of her bed where they had deposited the chest and stroked the carving lightly with her fingertips. She opened the trunk slightly and ran her hands across the imperfect stitches on the pillowcases from Ruth. Yes, she was sad for that girl, although the image was all but gone from her mind. She crawled back under her covers and gave a prayer of gratitude.

Time was nearing for the wedding. The fields were plowed, and the whole family helped lay the seed. The work went much faster when Robert was home for planting season. Unbelievably, everything was getting done. The women had time to set up another batch of cheese; even their goat Minnie was being unusually cooperative. Perhaps she enjoyed having Kyle for company late into the evenings as he continued to work on his final wedding day surprises and finishing touches to the house.

Helen had finished Claire's dress and was finishing up Ruth's. She chose to update one of her old dresses for herself with some of the techniques and details she had seen in the high fashion shops while in the city. Robert had a fine suit that he used for special occasions that he would wear. Helen made him a new tie out of some of the leftover material from Claire's light lavender gown. The men had bought Kyle a new suit and shoes when they were in the city and Helen fashioned him a matching tie, also from the lavender fabric.

One evening, Robert called a family meeting and announced that he and Mr. Orson had discussed it and agreed on making Kyle a partner on the ship *Helena*. He could eventually buy his own ship from his shares if that was what he and Claire decided was best and he could sail along with the *Helena*. He would learn more in the meantime under his father's guidance. They were to leave three weeks after the wedding. They would only be making a short trip, about three months out, he didn't want to tax the newlyweds by keeping them apart for too long at first (he added with a grin). Robert's last voyage was a long one; he was not eager himself to be away too long. That trip had brought in a very good profit allowing himself and his crew a little leeway.

The day of the wedding finally arrived. The hotel was full of guests and Mary, the bakery owner, offered a free breakfast for all the wedding guests. The sun was shining and it was promising to be a lovely spring day. Just warm enough for maybe a light sweater, with a gentle breeze coming in off the ocean bringing with it the scent of the lilac trees that were blooming in most of the yards just up from the shore.

There was room for all in the chapel sitting snugly in the pews. Kyle stood anxiously at the front with the minister, his stomach threatening to flop all the way over. He wasn't nervous, wondering if he had made the right choice. He knew without a doubt that he would adore Claire for the rest of their lives. No, he was excited to start their life and couldn't believe that day was finally here. He felt like he was just practicing being alive before he met Claire, and now his life was really going to begin. He jumped a little when the piano started the tune indicating the start of the ceremony; having been so lost in thought. He looked at his mom, sitting on the front bench. She was so beautiful and kind. He had always admired her and his dad's relationship. They had set a good example, and now it was his turn. She smiled up at her son and wiped her cheek. Kyle had to wipe his too. Then he saw a figure silhouetted at the front door. The early afternoon sun was shining behind his sister and above her, filtering through a round leaded and etched glass window, casting a golden glow inside the whole church.

Ruth looked so grown up in her simple flowing dress made of a rich green, the color of the leaves on the lilac trees that were lending their scent to the ceremony. She carried a small spray of lavender and chamomile flowers tied with a creamy silk ribbon. As she got closer, Kyle could see that she had pulled her hair up around the temples and let the rest hang loosely and curled. She gave him a big hug and he kissed her gently on her forehead like he always did and whispered, "I love you, my little Ruthie," and she took her place on the other side of the minister.

With the change of music everybody stood, facing the entrance. Silhouetted in the door was Claire, escorted by Robert. The veil and gauzy top layer of her gown gave the appearance she was glowing as the sunlight lit her from behind. She held on tight, her right arm looped through Robert's left, her hand on his forearm, his right hand resting on hers. He gave her hand a little tap, and she squeezed his arm to let him know she was ready. Her gown was simple yet elegant, made of two layers as they had seen in the city. The bottom layer was the lightest shade of lavender silk embossed with little flowers that one would only notice as the light hit it just so, falling just at the ankle so you could see the perfectly matching silk lavender flats. The top layer was similar to all the other dresses that Helen made with the scoop neck and waistline that fell just below the breast line; only the sleeves flowed in a sheer gauzy fabric capping long on her upper arm. The same sheer fabric was layered over the dress's bodice and finished below the knee. This sheer fabric gathered on the exposed chest and collar bones, tying at the neck with creamy silk ribbon like on the bouquets. Below the breast line lay Helen's signature embroidery on a wide strip of creamy silk ribbon. She had embroidered lavender and chamomile in iridescent threads. The veil was short in the front, just below Claire's chin, trailing long in the back, falling even with the gauzy layer of her dress.

A beaded headpiece that had been Helen's when she married Robert. Claire had tried to refuse, feeling that it should be Ruth who wore it at her wedding. But it was Ruth who had insisted, promising it would mean even more now when it was finally her turn to wear it.

Kyle had forgotten to breathe as Robert escorted Claire up the aisle. Claire had been looking down as she approached the front, now she looked up, lifting her head just slightly. She was grinning at Kyle through the veil despite herself. *This is it* she thought. *Who am I to be so blessed?*

Robert let go of Claire and turned to Kyle, holding him in a long embrace. "Breathe," he told his son and held him steady until he knew he had finally taken a solid breath. He then took Claire by the elbow, guiding her to her husband-to-be, stepping over to join his son, at his side of the altar, a witness to their union. He felt a tear trickle down his cheek as he looked lovingly at his own wife, thinking she was more beautiful now with wisdom in her eyes the years had brought. He looked over at his daughter, looking so much like a young woman, knowing how brave and kind and generous she was. And here was his son, his firstborn who had become such a righteous, honest, and hardworking man; standing at the altar with Claire, the miracle that was brought from the sea and foretold to him in a dream.

4

AFTER THE CEREMONY, most of the group joined the family in celebration at the Harrington's home. They had cleaned out the barn, and set up borrowed tables made of saw horses and planks of wood. The guests all hurriedly pitched in and started setting up a feast so fast you would have thought it magic. Everybody seemed to have a little something to add to the tables. They brought plates to eat off of so they could take them home and wash themselves, saving the family on clean-up duty after the party. There was music and dancing, toasts and tears. Mary had provided a beautiful layered cake for the couple. Everybody ooh'd and ah'd over the amazing cake. They had never seen such a cake before. It was covered in lilac and chamomile frosting flowers and strung with iridescent glass beads. Mary had seen a drawing of one in one of her supply catalogs, introducing the new fashion in wedding cakes, trying to sell the supplies needed to make one. Mary had the perfect opportunity to try it out, and it was a great success, although the guests were hesitant to cut into the work of art. The photographer got a picture of it for a keepsake. Kyle and Claire shared the first bites to put everyone at ease. It was as delicious as it was beautiful.

The festivities lasted well into the day. Now and then, a friend would bring them a gift to open and that gave the couple a chance to visit with everybody. As the day drew on, Robert noticed that he hadn't seen Mr. Orson. He thought he saw him at the back of the church during the ceremony and was commenting as such, when as if on cue, Mr. Orson came riding up atop a beautiful caramel-colored horse along with a gentleman in a delivery wagon (Claire had never seen Mr. Orson on a horse and it looked very a strange to her). He reached the party and took Kyle aside, seeming a bit uncomfortable, and whispered something to him. Kyle then went back to Robert leaving Mr. Orson to direct the delivery man towards the young couple's new home. It was then Kyle's turn to whisper to a curious Robert. By now, the whole crowd was hushed and curious.

Robert announced, "It seems Dale has brought a gift for the newlyweds and needs a bit of help with it. Any strapping young men out there willing to help? Good, yes, thank you. Everybody, please continue and we'll be right back!"

Kyle had made his way over to Claire. He apologized, saying this was not how he had planned it. He wanted to carry her over their threshold and privately enter their home together for the first time after everybody had left. But it seems that Mr. Orson was quite anxious to get his gift inside, and would she mind entering together now? Take a look around, then return to the party.

"Of course," she replied.

Kyle and Claire walked to the house, said their hello's to Mr. Orson, and stood there at the foot of their steps awkwardly, with Mr. Orson looking at them as if to say, "Well?" Robert pulled him aside and explained Kyle's request.

"Well, yes, of course." Mr. Orson replied, a little embarrassed and clearing his throat.

Kyle took Claire by the hand and led her up the stairs. He removed a sheet of canvas from in front of the new door, and hung where the plain plank door had been. This new door made Claire catch her breath. It was a beautiful oak door with a curved rod iron handle, latch, and hinges. The door itself was a piece of art. Kyle had carved, sanded, oiled, and buffed until the door was as smooth as glass. The image carved was of a giant oak tree with three little birds that looked like the sparrows Claire loved to watch flit around, flying around the top of the tree. Flowing from the background and around the front of the tree was a gentle creek, with grass swaying. In the foreground, bowing to drink from the creek was a graceful buck and his mate, closer to the base of the great tree looking out towards you as if in peaceful greeting.

"Oh, Kyle," were all the words Claire could summon.

Kyle opened the door and Claire started in, but Kyle grabbed her arm. "Wait!" he said, startling her a bit, and he swept her into his arms to carry her across the threshold. The crowd cheered and whistled from the barn, watching the scene from a respectful distance. Claire buried her head in Kyle's shoulder, laughing, embarrassed, and pleased simultaneously. Kyle gave her a long passionate kiss, met by more cheers and whistles before reluctantly lowering her to the ground. He wished everybody would just go home right now, but he knew he had to be gracious. Feeling a little dizzy, Claire had to hold onto Kyle for a moment while she got her bearings. They had shared a few kisses, stolen in the rare moments they were alone together, she felt as though she could never get enough of them. Kyle had never kissed her like this, the heat of his breath mixing with hers, wrapping her in a tremulous warmth. She was glad he was holding her, because she wasn't sure she would have been able to stand.

Looking around she saw their home, set up very much like Robert and Helen's as she remembered before she was banned; only Kyle had added his amazing woodwork everywhere Claire looked. That's what he had been working on in secret. There were carved moldings along the top of the walls, there was a staircase that led upstairs; only Kyle had fashioned theirs in a spiral. The railing was curved along with the spiral of the stairs. She could not imagine how he had accomplished that. Kyle led her by the hand into the kitchen, which was plain like their parents, no fancy carving; Claire thought that it was perfect. He then showed her the guest room (no furnishings at this time, they would fill it together). Then he took her to what she thought was maybe going to be the back porch, but when he opened the door and indicated for her to step through, she walked into a real bathroom. There was a toilet with its water tank high on the wall and the porcelain handle hanging from a chain, just like they had seen at the Spencers apartment. There was a built-in sink with a pump like in the elder Harrington's kitchen. And if that wasn't enough, to her left was a deep claw foot tub, a small potbelly stove at the foot to warm the room and heat the water they could pump from the sink right next to the tub. Claire was trembling and her eyes filled with tears. All she could do was hug Kyle. That's all he needed, his grin couldn't stretch much wider. As they left that room and returned to the kitchen, there was one more door under the stairs.

"Is that our room?" Claire asked as she was reaching for the crystal doorknob.

"Yes, but can we at least save that one for later?" Kyle asked, holding tightly to her hand.

"Of course" was her answer again as he pulled her to him for another long passionate kiss that left her knees wobbly.

Gathering themselves and taking a deep breath, they went back out to the, for once, patiently waiting, Mr. Orson.

Mr. Orson signaled to the delivery man, who pulled a large canvas off the contents waiting in the back of the wagon. You could hear a great intake of air from the whole crowd as he unveiled a large sofa. The sofa took four people to maneuver into the house. Luckily the door Kyle had made was larger than normal. They brought it into the living room and sat it beneath the far windows that overlooked the cliffs where Kyle asked Claire to marry him. Kyle and Claire, as well as all those in the house, just stood and stared silently for a long moment. The sofa was amazing. It was a good six feet long and fit perfectly beneath the windows as if Mr. Orson had measured. The overstuffed cushions were covered in lush red velvet, embossed with whimsical swirls. The arms of the piece rounded in big swooshing curves gathered at the front with large velvet buttons. The back curved elegantly, two smaller swells to each side of a slightly taller hump in the center. All this sat atop four large round wood balls, the same color as the carved front door.

Mr. Orson cleared his throat, misinterpreting the silence, saying, "If it is not to your liking of course I would gladly exchange it."

"No!" Claire and Kyle both exclaimed together.

"Oh Mr. Orson, it's beautiful. I've never seen anything like it. I love it, I truly love it." Claire assured him honestly.

"Yes Mr. Orson, it's very generous of you. It's fabulous." Kyle agreed, shaking Dale's hand vigorously.

"Yes, well, indeed." Mr. Orson returned, looking embarrassed and uncomfortable. "You've done a lovely job on your home, just lovely." He added, not actually looking around as he was heading for the door. Without stopping, he walked quickly to his horse riding back into town.

Most of the guests stayed until twilight. The crowd dwindled away a few at a time. Kyle and Claire had invited them to tour their home, knowing that they were probably very curious, especially about the gift from Mr. Orson. They all very respectfully stayed out of Claire and Kyle's bedroom, an unspoken respect that they were to be the first ones to enter there. When the final guests left and Claire went to help clean up, Helen swooshed her away with a wave of her hand, saying with a grin, "There will be no cleaning up for you out here tonight, dear. You and your husband go home. We'll bring you dinner tomorrow night and we do not expect to see you before then."

With many hugs and thanks, Claire and Kyle went to their home.

Claire's last surprise from Kyle, at least for this day, was their bedroom. On the bed laid the quilt she had received for her birthday and at the foot of the bed sat the chest. At the top of the bed was a headboard carved from the same wood as the front door. It was carved with more land-bound blackberries and two dragonflies. There was a matching armoire against the far wall beside a window that was covered in the lace curtains from the guest room that had been the only other home she knew.

"Kyle, you have given me so much. I don't have a gift for you," Claire whispered.

Kyle brought her to sit next to him on the bed and, with his hand stroking her cheek and tucking a loose hair behind her ear, whispered back, "You *are* my gift."

Part Three

What was it about this little girl that so easily and instantaneously cut through this man's narcissistic and unrelenting arrogance? From the very moment he laid eyes on her, a mere infant, he felt a jolt, a hint of awakening. It was from that moment that the little whisperings started and the world around him took on a different color. It was so subtle that he didn't even recognize it right away, but there it was, nonetheless.

Calypso gathers the fishing nets broken and lost by her land-bound children. Her offspring are drawn to the waters like a sick child to their mother's arms.

With ancient webbed fingers, she undoes a knot here, re-ties one there. She waits, she watches, patient and steady as the tides.

Calypso manipulates the nets, making them stronger and more beautiful, her vision reaching beyond our understanding.

1

"HAPPY BIRTHDAY MELANIE," Mr. Orson crooned, handing the sweet little birthday girl his gift.

Robert Harrington watched, quietly amazed at the transformation that had come over Mr. Orson, a long-time business partner in their import-export business. Dale Orson was known by most as a self-serving, bitter man, a man who held more interest in acquiring treasures and securing finances over anything. After he put his mind to the want of something, he stopped at nothing to obtain it. In these opinions of Mr. Orson, most would be correct. Robert himself would agree. About six years back, Dale Orson set his eyes on Melanie's mother, Claire. He wanted her for his own. Claire was a mysterious and beautiful young lady who had been saved from drowning by Kyle; Robert's son. Not recognizing the jealousy he felt of Robert's life, that was not all Dale coveted. He set his sights on Robert's ship, the 'Helena', and the land the Harrington home thrived on. Claire foiled Mr. Orson's plans to ruin Robert, his own business partner.

Nobody else in the small seaside town knew about the affair. The Harrington family handled it. Claire and the youngest Harrington, Ruthie, bravely and cleverly exposed Mr.

Orson's plan, but Robert and his wife Helen set the example of forgiveness, leaving Dale slightly humbled.

Nevertheless, nobody affected such a change in this man as little curly-haired, bright-eyed, 'three-year-old today' Miss Melanie; daughter of Claire and Kyle, granddaughter of Robert and Helen.

Little Miss Melanie clapped her hands as she plopped on the front steps of her grandparents' front porch. Mr. Orson sat beside her as she eagerly ripped the pretty paper off her gift. Melanie squealed in delight, running her delicate fingers over the embossed image on the front of her new book.

"Oh look, Poppy" she exhaled to her grandpa Robert, "look, it's Calwipso! She's under dat ship! Is she gonna sink dat ship, Gwumpy Dale? Can we wead it? Can we wead it now, Gwumpy Dale?"

Mr. Orson looked to Claire for guidance on this request. Dale could never deny this little treasure of a girl sitting beside him. He wanted to be the person Melanie saw in him.

"Perhaps you would like pie first? Then Daddy can play you a song on his violin, you and Poppy can have your birthday dance?" her mother answered, looking from Helen to Kyle for reassurance. She added, "Mr. Orson is welcome to stay and enjoy the rest of your party if he chooses. He can read you part of your new story before he goes?"

"YES, PIE! Anna song anna dance. Pwease Gwumpy Dale?"

Mr. Orson looked around uncomfortably, answering, "Uh-hum, well, of course," quietly adding, "thank you."

Turning from the kitchen sink where she had been anxiously keeping watch at the window, Helen threw the towel to the table as she ran towards the front door.

Ruth, walking up the path from town, ran towards her mother after seeing her burst through the front door, jumping down the front porch steps to meet her daughter.

"Oh Ruthie, let me look at you! My darling, you look well." Helen exclaimed, pulling out of her embrace to examine her daughter, now a beautiful young woman herself.

Both mother and daughter turned and laughed as they heard the squeal of "Auntie Rue!" following the slam of Kyle and Claire's front door being thrown open by the very enthusiastic and quick five-year-old Melanie.

Melanie came running full speed, her dark curls bouncing wild and long on one side of her head. The other side was braided and neatly held by a green ribbon that matched her eyes. Shaking her head, following close behind was Claire, abandoned brush in one hand and the second green ribbon in the other.

"Auntie Rue! You're back from school!" Melanie declared.

"I couldn't miss my favorite niece's fifth birthday could I?" teased Ruth.

"Daddy and Poppy won't be here," Melanie explained, producing her very best sad lower lip. "They are still at sea… I want to be at sea but daddy says I have to wait until I am bigger than the fish, but I AM bigger than the fish! I won't even fit in the roaster pan."

"Well, I'm glad you're not at sea so we can have a party for your birthday. Just us girls this year," Ruth added with some belly tickles, making Melanie giggle away her pouty lip. Then serious again, Melanie clarified,

"And Grumpy Dale! Mommy, Grumpy Dale will come to my party, right?"

"Yes, Melanie," Claire answered as they reached her in-laws' front porch. "Sit now and let me finish your hair, then we can all get ready for your party." Melanie sat exaggeratedly on the porch steps as Ruth and Helen continued into the house.

"Melanie is still saying 'Grumpy Dale'? Shouldn't we correct her?" Ruth inquired with a grin.

"It's the funniest thing, Ruthie, Melanie insists on calling Mr. Orson her grandpa Dale even though we've explained that he is just a friend and not actually her grandpa. Not like Poppy is her grandpa. But she just says in her precocious way, 'I know that! Poppy is my Poppy and Grumpy is my Grumpy.' We've apologized to Mr. Orson and tried to work with Melanie to say grandpa more clearly, but Mr. Orson insists he doesn't mind.

And you know?" Helen continues, "I don't believe he does. He seems to honestly like it! It's the funniest thing; I believe that little girl has found a soft spot in old 'Grumpy'. Funny little girl."

"Will you read from my story of Calypso again, Grumpy Dale?" Melanie implored her party guest, to which Mr. Orson unsurprisingly replied, as they sat together on the velvety plush red couch in Kyle and Claire's living room. It had been a very lavish and generous wedding gift from Mr. Orson.

"As long as it is agreeable with your mother, I could stay to read a couple more pages from where we left off. Where were we?"

"Calypso was listening at the side of the ship, and she's going to stir up a storm to tip it right over!" Melanie replied in great animation.

"Yes, yes, very good. I do believe you could recite the entire story to me by now madam." Mr. Orson complimented.

Claire thought she saw the hint of a smile on Mr. Orson's face as he started to read to Melanie, surprising her out of her thoughts while clearing up the dishes. Melanie loved everything about the sea and was particularly taken with Calypso. Claire appreciated that Melanie only wanted Grumpy Dale to read her this particular story. This story gave Claire a peculiar feeling of déjà vu she couldn't explain, although she tried to explain it away by reasoning that it was just her usual worry over Kyle and Robert being out to sea.

2

CLAIRE AND HELEN KEPT their little homestead running while the men were away. Helen had kept the farm running with the help of Kyle and Ruth for the last few years, tending their chickens, Rose the milk cow, Minnie the goat, and their mare, Sunrise. Then there was tending the garden through the seasons, making the goat milk soap and cheeses they sold at the summer market. Not to mention Helen's embroidered nightgowns and linens that are always in demand.

Now with Kyle captain of his own vessel and Ruthie away at university, coming home only on school breaks, the work was down to the two ladies of their respective households.

Mr. Orson checked in often, occasionally hiring local youth to help at the Harrington farm when something unforeseen or more challenging arose. Robert always arranged for extra help to be available during his absence, but life often surprises you, and you can't always plan for everything.

Although the women recognized the change in Mr. Orson, it was still hard for them to accept his help or trust his motives. Mr. Orson helped anyway. Melanie was always thrilled to see her Grumpy Dale. He patiently listened to her stories and admired her latest artwork.

Often Melanie would walk along the shoreline with Mr. Orson at her side, looking for the little brown crabs that scuttled from rock to rock. Claire walked nervously at the water's edge between her daughter and the shoreline.

Unlike her mother, Melanie had no fear of the water and loved to swim, no matter the weather or appropriate attire. Only twice in recent years, the fearless fish of a girl ran directly into the ocean catching her mother off guard. Claire pulled her confused daughter quickly to the shore with the strongest reprimand.

"But momma, didn't you hear her? She called me to play." Was Melanie's reasoning upon her mother's panicked questioning and scolding.

After the second incident, Melanie was forbidden to go into the water without her father. She was quite assured by her mother that her strolls along the shore, even with Grumpy Dale, would come to an abrupt halt if she did not obey the newly placed rule.

Claire had never become completely comfortable around the water since the day Kyle brought her to the safety of the shore. Anything before that day was still a blank, just occasional glimpses of the ghost of a life that didn't ever seem quite real. Visions of a spoiled girl with adoring parents, feet flying overboard, little red fish, and tall white wigs. Sometimes, she was taken aback, seeing the young girl in her visions reflected back at her as she watched her own daughter.

Melanie spotted her father's ship from the lookout where their property ended in a cliff with a downward path leading to a small inlet below. When the tide allowed, they would make their way down the path to picnic and look for small 'treasures' that washed ashore. Gifts from Calypso herself, Melanie was convinced.

After hearing the news that Kyle's ship was returning, Melanie had camped out for the majority of the last three days, keeping vigil. This had been the longest time her dad had been away, and it had been over a year and he would be home for her eighth birthday. Kyle and Robert had been out for her seventh birthday and Papa would possibly just miss this one too. But her daddy would be home.

Recognizing the flag atop the mast with the company insignia and colors that announced ownership of the vessel, Melanie dropped her biscuit, forgotten for the seagulls, and ran with all her might yelling to her mother and grandmother that her daddy's ship was coming.

It would still be a couple of hours before Kyle's ship would pull into port and be taxied to the dock, another hour or so before Kyle himself stepped onto shore.

Melanie struggled with her impatience as she waited for Claire and Helen to finish up their chores, clean up, and walk to town. Finally arriving in town, Melanie ran ahead to Mr. Orson's place of business, where he resided on the upper two floors, wanting Grumpy Dale to share in her excitement.

Claire was relieved to see Melanie pulling Mr. Orson down the street. This meant she didn't need to enter the building. Any time she could avoid it, she would. The memory of her time there with Ruth, uncovering the stolen ledgers, still sent a small shiver down her spine.

As was tradition, Kyle, being captain, was the last to leave the ship, allowing the crew to greet awaiting friends and family first. Watching the crew disembark seemed to take as long as the trip itself.

Kyle could feel the heat behind his eyes as they started to well; his stomach was swimming like it never did at sea. He remembered being on the other side of this, on the shore, waiting for *his* father to return, walking down the plank onto the dock.

There they were, the amazing women of his life. Wife, daughter, mother. Barely giving him time to register their beautiful faces, Melanie ran to meet him on the dock, hurtling herself into his arms, burying her face into his neck, salt from their tears mixing from the salt from the sea.

3

"BUT DADDY, MOMMA, I'm ten years old now. I won't get underfoot, I promise!" Melanie implored her parents. "I'll mop the decks! Help in the galley! I'm a big help to you, momma, and grandma." Taking a breath looking between her parents for any sign of hope, she added, "Daddy, I'm bigger than most of the fish you bring home for dinner. You said."

Kyle had to grin at that and conceded, "This is a big decision Melanie, your mother and I will have to discuss it at length."

Not quite ready to give up on arguing her case quite yet, Melanie added, "Papa said you were ten the first time you went out with him." She may have overstepped with that comment and after seeing the look on her mother's face; Melanie thought it best to drop it for now. After a most awkward second, Melanie decided hugs were always a good way to leave things, so she quickly hugged her parents and ran upstairs to clean her room like her mother had been asking for three days.

Over the next two weeks, Kyle and Claire discussed allowing Melanie to go, weighing the good, the bad, the ups and downs. Melanie was sure to be especially helpful with all the chores around the homestead. She only had to be asked maybe twice to clean her messes or feed the chickens before dark.

Kyle and Claire were working in the garden with Robert and Helen getting the last of the seeding done. While working, they continued the ongoing discussion concerning the prudence of allowing Melanie to travel with her father. It was the best time of year to be at sea, with mostly mild weather conditions on this particular route. Melanie was sure to learn and love everything about being on a ship, but she could be impetuous, and Kyle wouldn't be able to keep an eye on her at all times and he couldn't ask his crew members to undertake that responsibility. For the safety of the ship's occupants, the crew had their tasks to attend to.

Ruth, being home after finishing university and putting her degree to good use acting as an unofficial local veterinarian, came around the corner after helping Melanie with the chickens.

"I was thinking," Ruth started as she approached her family, looking behind her to make sure Melanie had gone in to check the stew as she had asked her, "I know I was never interested in going out on the ship when I was younger, but maybe I could go along and take care of Melanie. It would be a great opportunity for me to do some field studies. I haven't said anything to Melanie."

"What about your veterinarian work?" her mother, Helen inquired.

"It's just a short trip this time mom, Randy Hayes' boy, Andrew has been helping me out, apprenticing I guess, but he has a real knack for it. He could see to my regular rounds. I'll have time to check on all my patients before I go. It should be fine. Everybody managed without a vet before." Ruth reasoned out, unsure if she was trying to convince herself or the family.

That was a fair solution. So it was decided, Claire being the least enthusiastic about it.

4

AS CLAIRE'S APPREHENSION GREW, Melanie's excitement grew along with it. It was finally time to go. Melanie and Ruth's new trunks were packed with everything they could possibly need, their respective mothers apprehensive about their girls embarking for the first time. Both girls took plenty of paper and writing utensils. Ruth planned to sketch the animals and take as many notes as she could, Melanie planned on drawing everything she saw and writing all the stories she was sure she would be inspired to write.

Riding in the wagon bright and early, Ruth was already turning green with nerves about going on the ship. Although trying not to show it and adding to her mother's worries, Helen of course saw and placed a calming hand on her daughter's knee. Melanie in contrast, could hardly sit for her excitement and fell to the deck of the wagon more than once as it bumped over ruts in the road, but nothing could dampen her enthusiasm. Claire had to laugh despite her worry.

With hugs and goodbyes taken care of, the families of the crew waved their arms and handkerchiefs, if they had them, from the shore. As the ship was being ferried out to deeper water, the crew had a moment to wave back to their loved ones until they set to work on sailing the 'Claire 2' to the ports ahead. Claire gasped as she spotted Kyle grabbing their daughter, stopping her from climbing on the side rails for more enthusiastic waving. Standing a little farther down the shore, Dale Orson also gasped, adding under his breath, "Calypso, keep her safe."

Being at sea was everything Melanie had thought it would be. She loved the smell of the ocean, the salty air on her cheeks, and the sound of the wind when it made the sails dance. The rhythm of the ship as it rocked on the waves brought her comfort like rocking on her Papa's lap on the front porch swing. Ruth on the other hand was struggling to get her sea legs, spending much of her first days laying in bed where she and Melanie's shared quarters. Melanie tried to be patient with Ruth's suffering but more often than not, she would tiptoe off to explore when Ruth was able to doze off, scaring Ruth when she woke to see her gone. The fear would momentarily chase the sickness away as she shot up the stairs to the upper decks, inevitably finding Melanie following one of the sailors, asking questions, or helping to tie up ropes, or checking charts with her father.

If all else failed, Ruth knew she would find Melanie at the portside bow as she did early one morning, about a week into their travels. Walking up behind Melanie, Ruth looked around to see who her niece was talking to, laughing and clapping. There was nobody there except Melanie, who exclaimed in dismay as a pod of rambunctious dolphins swam away, "AHHH, Auntie Rue! You scared them away! They were dancing to that song!"

"Okaaay, um, I'm sorry Melanie, but you know you aren't supposed to be up here by yourself," Ruth replied wearily.

To which Melanie reasoned quite matter-of-fact, "But she won't sing if someone else is here." As if that was the most reasonable retort.

Another week passed and Ruth was finally feeling better, getting used to the rocking, she hardly noticed it anymore. She kept herself busy reorganizing Kyle's filing and improving on the inventory coding system her brother had in place. Melanie stayed with her, most of the time, alongside her dad on the bridge, copying the maps, and star charts into her notebooks, humming an eerie tune neither Ruth nor Kyle was familiar with. It made the hair on Kyle's neck stand on end as she started adding words to the tune. She sang:

Do not fear my darlings dry

You are never far from my watching eyes

Come to me at the water's edge

Dare to dive its depths

I am here and will keep you safe

Fathoms below or skies above

With two weeks' travel and one stop behind them, the final port before returning home was just two more days before them. They would stay at port for three to four days as was usual and return straight home. The weather had been cooperative and if it continued they would be home in two weeks.

Being back on shore was a relief to Ruth and a great annoyance to Melanie. It took all of Ruth's creativity to cajole Melanie away from the docks to explore inland. Melanie did love to see the unusual animals and draw them in her notebook alongside her Auntie Rue. She found that the language barrier was not as big a problem for the children as it was for the adults. She made friends easily in the village and played a fun game kicking a ball made from a stuffed wild boar's belly. She would have to teach this to Grumpy Dale when they returned home, she thought to herself, giggling at the imagined sight of it.

Finally, the time to head home was upon them. Ruth was distressed about leaving but made plans to return and study with a veterinarian here when she could arrange it. She thought of her friend William Marshall who had trained as a doctor in the city. He had been quite influential in encouraging her to attend university for veterinary studies. Ruth thought surely William would be fascinated with the herbal remedies and treatments used by the people here.

Melanie was happy to be back on the ship and was determined to sail with her father as often as she could convince her parents to allow it.

Only two days traveling home and Kyle could see signs of a storm on the horizon. He paced the parameter of the ship trying to get a feel for the wind and gauge whether or not this storm was going to be an issue for them or if they could skirt it. Approaching the portside bow, Kyle could see Melanie and Ruth. Ruth was attempting to tame Melanie's hair in braids as Melanie was singing that haunting tune again:

Do not fear my darlings dry

You are never far from my watching eyes

Come to me at the water's edge

Dare to dive its depths

I am here and will keep you safe

Fathoms below or skies above

You are secured within my love

Kyle could not explain it, but that song gave him the shivers. Approaching the girls he asked Melanie how she knew this song, she answered "The ocean has been teaching me." As if it was a matter of fact.

A brisk snap of the previously gentle pulling sails drew Kyle away from further questioning; the ribbon Ruth was tying to the end of Melanie's braid flew from her fingers, all three watched it swirl away, momentarily caught by its motion.

"You two get below to your cabin. Quickly. And stay there." Kyle ordered his daughter and sister before turning his attention to the crew, the ship, and the sudden storm upon them.

Huddled below in their cabin Ruth was feeling sicker by the moment as the wind continued to grow and build, bringing with it larger and stronger waves rocking the ship menacingly. In the darkness of their cabin, Melanie tried to ignore the song calling to her from outside, from the darkened ocean. Above the shouts from the courageous men working to ride the storm, securing the safety of the crew, the ship, and cargo, above the sound of her poor Auntie Rue's retching, there was the persistence of that song.

Between bouts of retching, Ruth would try to comfort her little niece who sat next to her, taking her anxiety as fear. Melanie sat with her back against the wall, occasionally reaching over to rub her Aunties back, knees folded up, singing that song she had taken to singing.

Melanie was torn between obeying her father, caring for Ruth, and that darn song calling louder and louder until she no longer heard anything else. Without thought, she rose and climbed up the lilting stairs to the deck up above and to the call she no longer had the power to ignore.

After another gut-wrenching heave, Ruth noticed the absence of Melanie's song.

"Mel? Mel!" was Ruth's panicked yell as she looked around the small room to find her niece. She knew exactly where to find her as she struggled up the stairs towards the portside bow, the rocking of the ship, her pounding head, and bitter sea sickness making it necessary for her to crawl, barely taking notice of the crew as they struggled to stay upright and navigate the storm. Relentless waves were crashing over the sides of the ship, the winds whipping her hair across her face but there Melanie was, just as Ruth had suspected; until she wasn't. Quick as Ruth could yell Melanie's name, the ship tipped aggressively portside like a teapot trying to empty itself of its contents, taking Melanie with it.

Kyle looked over just as Melanie's feet disappeared over the side; three other crew members were already on their way over to help retrieve the girl.

Shocked by the cold, Melanie snapped out of her trance and was able to take in her situation. *'I'm in the water,* ' she realized, surprised but unafraid as the waters pulled her and stirred her around like a carrot in her mother's stew. "Yes, I know your mother, child," she thought she heard as the grip of the water pulled her towards the barnacle-covered underbelly of her father's ship.

The waves were too wild for Kyle or the crew to get a fix on Melanie, the ship lifting too high then too low, the sky unnaturally dark from the storm.

Melanie gasped from the sharp pain as her back scraped across the barnacles attached to the dark wooden bottom of the ship. Her eyes closed, her sight faded to murky black, secure in the sensation of being lifted like a babe cradled in large strong hands, into; nothing.

Upon opening her eyes, Melanie saw the giant face she knew from her stories and dreams. Her skin was a silvery green; her long hair flowed out around her moving sinuously with the water's currents. Fish were swimming in and out of her curls. Her face was wild and beautiful with large round eyes, being a completely glassy silver with a slit of a metallic black pupil, not a bit of white. She smiled with a mouth slightly too wide for her face exposing a row of sharp teeth. Calypso.

Calypso cradled Melanie to her chest while shifting from the size of a Blue Whale to about the same size as Melanie's mother, stroking Melanie's dark curls that had come free from the braids. A myriad of fish circled the two in celebratory swirls of confetti bubbles.

Feeling helpless and desperate after trying unsuccessfully to spot his daughter within the roiling waters for what seemed like hours or possibly only minutes, Kyle fell to his knees, pleading to Calypso to return his beloved daughter. Barely believing his words as he was not a superstitious man, as the wind subsided and the water calmed, in his mind he heard,

I am here and will keep you safe

Fathoms below or skies above

You are secured within my love

"THERE!" A crew member spotted her limp body as it bobbed to the surface on the opposite side of the ship from where she toppled over. Without waiting, he tied himself to the safety rope and dove in. Kyle was at the side of the ship before they could even hear the splash, along with Ruth and four other crew members. As soon as the rescuer had Melanie secured, they all pulled the rope with its passengers to the security of the ship's deck.

Kyle quickly turned his daughter on her side to try and expel the water from her lungs. "Not again, not again. Come on, breath. " he whispered urgently, readying to turn Melanie to her back and start chest compressions, as she suddenly spluttered, coughed to clear her lungs, and whispered back "Daddy?" before passing out.

Getting Melanie cleaned up and dried, Kyle found the heavy scraping across his daughter's little back caused by the barnacles. The wounds were deep and inflamed. Melanie was in and out of consciousness with fever, sleeping restlessly on Kyle's bed in his cabin. Ruth tried what she could from the limited herbs and treatments carried aboard the ship, but she was a vet, not a doctor. She was able to bring the fever down but the results were always temporary and Melanie would slip back into delirium and fever, waking just long enough to mutter "Don't worry daddy, she sent me back." or "She got small, then big and brought me back." Her eyes would flutter halfway open and she'd grin saying, "Silly fish".

Neither Kyle nor Ruth would leave Melanie's side. O'Connell, the unofficial ship's cook, brought them their meals, and broth for Melanie. Kyle's second in command, Franklin, saw to bringing the ship safely home. The weather was cooperative and they had a steady wind that got them home in one and a half weeks; sooner than would have been expected, gratefully.

Claire had been restless and full of worry for the last week and a half. She was ready for her family to be home and couldn't shake the knot in her stomach. It was all she could do to just keep busy.

Looking out across the cliff that looked out to the sea, at the end of their property for probably the twentieth time that day, Claire dropped her bucket of goat milk from the reluctant Minnie and ran to Helen and Robert's home on their shared property.

Bursting through the door, white as a ghost, she informed Helen that they needed to hitch the cart and head to town; Kyle's ship was just about here. Seeing the look on Claire's face, Helen did not argue. Normally they would walk to meet the men who preferred to walk home after being at sea. And normally there wasn't a feeling of urgency, knowing it could take a few hours to get the ship ferried to the docks.

Reaching town and guiding the horse as close to the docks as possible; Helen noticed Mr. Orson uncharacteristically rushing to the docks as well, as the 'Claire 2' was being ferried in sooner than expected. There weren't any other ships in the queue at the moment.

Claire jumped from the carriage before it came to a full stop rushing to get to the ship; the final mooring seemed to take ages. Having secured the horse, Helen came to stand with Claire just as Claire's knees buckled upon seeing Kyle quickly descending the plank, Ruth right behind him, the burden in Kyle's hand easily recognizable by the flow of dark curls cascading off their daughter's head against Kyle's shoulder.

After panicked questions and reassurances that Melanie was still alive but very ill, the family rushed home. Mr. Orson, who himself was torn between following the Harrington family to be with Melanie, waved Kyle off, telling him not to worry about the ship. He would see to the practicalities of docking and unloading protocol. Flushed from running and being unaccustomed to high emotion, Mr. Orson boarded the ship, an unfamiliar feeling of shame washing over him as he remembered the last time he traversed this plank, to board Robert's ship to steal inventory books so many years ago.

5

HELEN HAD BEEN TRYING every tried and true remedy she knew of for three days since they returned. Melanie was less restless and sleeping more peacefully. The wounds on her back from the barnacles continued to ooze and were still inflamed, making it necessary to keep her on her side or stomach. She would wake briefly and smile at whoever was taking a turn sitting with her, but her fever was not dropping past a certain point. On the fourth day, she woke long enough to ask for Grumpy Dale. Kyle fetched him immediately.

Mr. Orson rode back on his horse right away and spent the whole day at her side reading her stories though she slept and telling her about how he had framed her art and where he had it hanging in his library. He told her about a beautiful new fabric he'd seen in one of the shops in town, thinking he might buy a bit of it so Helen could make her a new dress for when she was feeling better. He told her about the pod of dolphins he saw dancing just past the docks as he was sitting on the deck outside his library having his afternoon tea.

Claire came into the room to check on them once again, bringing broth for Melanie, and again to offer Mr. Orson something to eat, of which he had so far refused any offers. She cleared her throat softly, Mr. Orson had fallen asleep, bent over with his forehead resting at Melanie's side, her little hand in his. Mr. Orson jumped as Claire lay the broth on the side table. His eyes were red and swollen, his signature fishtail kerchief askew in his usually immaculate suit pocket, his customarily perfect pompadour white hair lay flattened and out of kilter.

"I was just going to see if I could persuade a little broth down her." Claire introduced to try and ease Mr. Orson's obvious discomfort.

"Yes," he grumbled, clearing his throat, adding another "Yes." staring through Claire as he said it. Dale then stood abruptly, pulling his jacket front down with more force than necessary as if to emphasize his abrupt statement of "This just won't do."

Mr. Orson turned sharply and walked out of the house.

Ruth was quite surprised to see Mr. Orson standing at the door of Claire and Kyle's home. He had left abruptly three days before, and the word was he had gone out of town. Then she noticed William Marshal standing with Mr. Orson. Feeling a bit flustered, Ruth ran her hands along her rumpled dress and hair, untidy from a night at Mel's side, having taken a shift so Kyle and Claire could rest. Ruth managed to squeak out, "Um, err, uh" as Claire joined them at the door.

It had been some time since Ruth had seen William, from the time when she finished veterinarian training and returned home. He had been very kind and attentive while she lived in the city. Although she had friends, Olivia and Bart that she stayed with, William had helped her through some of her studies and navigate city life, introducing her to his group of friends at college. The group included her in many of their outings to plays, art showings, and musical performances.

Breaking Ruth's moment of awkward staring, Claire exclaimed, "Why William!" looking between him and Mr. Orson in puzzlement. "So good to see you, but... Oh please, do come in, come in."

Striding towards the living room, Mr. Orson made to sit on the opulent red couch, bent to sit, stood, and bent again, finally deciding to stand. Relieved he had made a decision, they all followed suit.

"What can I do for you, William?" Claire asked.

"I'm here about Melanie." William clarified, "Mr. Orson came to me and explained the situation. He believed I could be of help. And so do I."

Mr. Orson remembered something Mr. Marshal had said on his last visit to the bank Mr. Orson owned. They were finishing the deposit transaction from Mr. Marshal's latest wheat harvest, and Mr. Marshal was bragging about his son William 'The Doctor' once again, to Mr. Orson's great annoyance. It had registered with Dale in a flash; William was on a team at the Advanced Studies Medical Center, testing a new medication showing great promise in treating infection and fever.

Kyle returned home shortly after Mr. Orson and William had arrived. Kyle had reluctantly gone to town to attend to a couple of items of business on the ship. On his return, the family gathered at Kyle and Claire's, along with Mr. Orson and William.

William explained about the experimental medication his team was developing. So far, the tests and limited treatments have shown promise. Having examined Melanie, he was confident in the hope for good results.

Kyle was grateful for his mother's calm presence as they sat quietly running through their thoughts concerning the decision they were about to make in a new territory they felt so uneducated about. Ruth shared her little knowledge from what she had gleaned during her schooling. At that time, the medication was only in early development. Kyle wished his father had returned from his trade route. He was not due home for three more months. Kyle longed for his steady council.

In their contemplative silence, William interjected, "As far as costs, it's um," stammering, he cast a quick glance towards Mr. Orson, who had been entirely quiet throughout. The family caught the slightest shake of Mr. Orson's head as William continued "… taken care of."

The Doctor squeezed a thick liquid from a short syringe towards the back of Melanie's throat as Claire held her upright against her chest.

"This might make her nauseous," William warned, "but continue to give this to her three times a day until it is all gone. Even when her fever breaks and she seems to be getting better. It is important to continue with the medication until it is finished. As soon as you can get her to eat again, give her the meds after she has something on her stomach, which will help with nausea."

Holding her daughter and feeling hope as she stroked her daughter's sweaty curls, Claire smiled as Ruth studiously took notes as William explained about the medication while applying a salve and clean bandages to Melanie's back.

Mr. Orson excused himself as Helen invited the men to stay for lunch. William glanced at Ruth, who blushed, and he accepted gladly.

Ruth and William sat at the table for two more hours, talking excitedly about new medical breakthroughs. Ruth continued to take notes, finally walking him to the trailhead that led to his father's home.

William came every day to check on Melanie. By the second day, Melanie's fever spiked and she vomited wretched dry heaves. The woman changed out her bedding and nightdress she had sweat through. William cleaned and applied more salve and clean bandages to her back. Kyle paced below the stairs that led to her room, finally retiring to the barn to work on carving the intricate design encircling the rim of the cedar chest he was commissioned to do. Feeling absolutely helpless, he had to keep busy.

William reassured them that this was to be expected. Hopefully, after this crisis passed, she would be well on the mend.

On day three, Claire was awoken by Melanie gently tapping the top of her mother's head. Claire had fallen asleep again at her daughter's side. Looking at her daughter's bright open eyes, she heard her sweet little voice rasp out, "Momma, I'm thirsty." The most beautiful sentence Claire had heard in a long time.

Day four, Melanie's appetite had returned and Grumpy Dale was summoned for the reading of stories, for which he gladly obliged.

Epilogue

WILLIAM STAYED TWO MORE WEEKS after Melanie's fever broke, visiting often to check on Melanie's progress. After concluding that Melanie was indeed progressing beautifully, he lingered, helping Ruth with milking the cow and goat, feeding the chickens, and going on her rounds to check on the neighbor's animals.

Between stories, Mr. Orson read to Melanie. Melanie sang him her new song and told him fantastic tales from under the sea. When he inquired how she came up with such great tales, Melanie told him quite frankly, "They are from when I was between here and there."

William needed to return to the medical center and deliver his report about the medications' success. It was his last night in town, and Claire and Helen were on the porch of the junior Harrington home, sharing a knowing smile as they watched Ruth walk William to the trailhead.

Mr. Orson joined them on the porch after visiting Melanie once again. The women turned towards him. Mr. Orson, his white hair more modestly poufed, his fishtail kerchief a humble shade of blue, pulled down his jacket front and proclaimed, "Yes, well. Ahem. I believe this town needs its own medical clinic. Yes. Doctor Marshal is a fine man. Yes."

Mr. Orson stepped off the porch and walked back home.

He made sure that was exactly what happened.

About the Author

PATTY GLASER is a newly published author after a long career as a stay home mom and chief go-to volunteer of all things church and children.

Patty has been married to her high school sweetheart for forty years. Thirty of those years have been spent in their current home, with no plans of leaving any time soon. They have raised their three amazing children together and have been further blessed with five grandchildren.

Finding herself an empty nester, Patty has been able to set the ever-present characters bumping around in her mind to the page. When she is not writing, she is creating original works of art, refinishing furniture, sewing, knitting, crocheting… basically anything artsy. Patty, also known as Nana to her grandchildren, loves to pass on her love of creativity to her grandchildren with impromptu crafts and art projects.